"Humble, aren't you?"

David glanced across the bed at Courtney. "Haven't you heard? Arrogance is a prerequisite for doctors."

"I hadn't heard—nor had I seen it up close and personal."

Despite the words coming out of her mouth, David couldn't help but stare. If she didn't have the sexiest lips he'd ever seen, he'd turn in his stethoscope and put himself out to pasture.

"You work at the gift shop—not directly with doctors?"

"That's right, I don't."

He'd swear her pride had taken a hit. Something in her eyes dimmed, some inner spark that was struggling to burn all but sputtered and went out.

He wasn't sure what he'd said, but he wanted to fix it—even though he had tried fixing things for a woman once and it hadn't gone well.

The sooner he got out of Walnut River, the better.

Dear Reader,

If we don't know where we came from, we don't know who we are, and family is the framework of our identity. I inherited a way with words from my father, but unfortunately, he didn't live to see my first book. I've always wondered about his reaction.

In *Paging Dr. Daddy,* David Wilder is estranged from his father whose death robs him of the chance to mend fences. He'll never know whether or not his charity work redeemed past mistakes and made his father proud. But I was able to give my hero closure to that question. For myself, I have to imagine that wherever my dad is, he's smiling with paternal pride for the daughter who loves writing as much as he did.

It was a pleasure to work with all the authors who participated in this continuity, five talented ladies with whom I formed a sort of family bond. Many thanks to our editor and "mother hen," Susan Litman, who nurtured us through bringing our characters to life.

Enjoy!

Teresa Southwick

PAGING
DR. DADDY

TERESA SOUTHWICK

SPECIAL EDITION®

Published by Silhouette Books

America's Publisher of Contemporary Romance

Special thanks and acknowledgment are given
to Teresa Southwick for her contribution to
THE WILDER FAMILY series.

 SILHOUETTE BOOKS

ISBN-13: 978-0-373-24886-5
ISBN-10:   0-373-24886-5

PAGING DR. DADDY

Books by Teresa Southwick

Silhouette Special Edition

The Summer House #1510
  "Courting Cassandra"
Midnight, Moonlight &
  Miracles #1517
It Takes Three #1631
§§*The Beauty Queen's Makeover* #1699
At the Millionaire's Request #1769
‡*Paging Dr. Daddy* #1886

Silhouette Romance

Wedding Rings and
  Baby Things #1209
The Bachelor's Baby #1233
A Vow, a Ring, a Baby Swing #1349
The Way to a Cowboy's Heart #1383
And Then He Kissed Me #1405
With a Little T.L.C. #1421
The Acquired Bride #1474
Secret Ingredient: Love #1495
The Last Marchetti Bachelor #1513
**Crazy for Lovin' You* #1529
**This Kiss* #1541
**If You Don't Know by Now* #1560
**What If We Fall in Love?* #1572
Sky Full of Promise #1624
†*To Catch a Sheik* #1674
†*To Kiss a Sheik* #1686
†*To Wed a Sheik* #1696

Silhouette Books

The Fortunes of Texas:
  Shotgun Vows

††*Baby, Oh Baby* #1704
††*Flirting with the Boss* #1708
††*An Heiress on His*
  Doorstep #1712
§*That Touch of Pink* #1799
§*In Good Company* #1807
§*Something's Gotta Give* #1815

*The Marchetti Family
**Destiny, Texas
†Desert Brides
††If Wishes Were…
§Buy-a-Guy
‡The Wilder Family
§§Most Likely To…

TERESA SOUTHWICK

lives with her husband in Las Vegas, the city that reinvents itself every day. An avid fan of romance novels, she is delighted to be living out her dream of writing for Silhouette Books.

To Robert Magnus Johnson, who took time out from "the law stuff" to answer my questions about the Servicemen's Group Life Insurance.
And you thought I was joking about dedicating this book to you. Thanks for your help, Bob.

Chapter One

She would beg, borrow, lie, cheat or steal for her child.

Courtney Albright knew what she had to do was one notch down from all of the above, but for her it was worse in some ways. She needed a favor from a man she had no reason to trust. Dr. David Wilder, genius plastic surgeon, lousy family guy. She supposed it made sense that a man empty and hollow enough to ignore and neglect the people who loved him would dedicate himself to enhancing outer beauty.

The problem was she'd just had an accident with her daughter in the car. Janie's face was broken and the doctors here in Walnut River were saying they didn't have the specialized skills she needed. David Wilder did and he'd agreed to a consult. It was a favor and Courtney didn't trust favors. Especially from men.

But her little girl was lying in a hospital bed with half her face covered in gauze bandages and fallout from a favor was a small price to pay for her little girl's health. So where was he? What was taking so long? Maybe he wouldn't show up.

With every ounce of willpower she possessed, Courtney held back the sob that pushed up from deep inside and lodged in her throat. Tears wouldn't help—they never had and never would. Especially not now. To get through this crisis, her six-year-old needed strength, not a mother who ran away. Hysterics would be like running away, and she couldn't give in to that. Her own mother had just taken off without a word. Courtney had had her father, such as he was. But Janie's father was dead. Janie only had *her* and she'd do her best not to let her baby down.

At least not again.

The accident was bad enough. And if she could, she would trade places with Janie in a heartbeat. Courtney had a bump on the head and a broken wrist, but that was nothing compared to what her little girl was suffering. Courtney had refused to let them admit her as a patient. She'd insisted they let her be with Janie. Hospitals were scary. She worked here, but not in patient care.

"Mrs. Albright?"

At the sound of the deep voice, Courtney glanced over her shoulder. It was him—David Wilder. He was really here and, if possible, more handsome than the one and only time she'd seen him. She shuddered with relief although it shamed her. She hated needing something from him or anyone else. But she'd have hated it more if he'd blown her off.

"You're here. I didn't think you'd…" She pressed her lips together, cutting off what she'd been about to say. "Thank you for coming, Dr. Wilder."

"You know me?" he asked.

"I saw you at your father's funeral."

James Wilder had died of a heart attack not quite two months ago and Courtney still missed him. He was the only man she'd ever known who had been kind to others without expecting anything in return.

"There were a lot of people there." David frowned as if he was thinking back.

He was a famous Beverly Hills plastic surgeon to the stars so there had been a lot of talk about him that day. About him in the tabloids, linked to A-list movie actresses. About him featured on TV gossip shows in regard to cosmetic procedures on models. Him dating a bevy of beautiful, high-profile women for about a minute until he moved on.

The Dr. David Wilder could be in the movies himself. Dark hair meticulously mussed, vivid blue eyes. Square jaw with some serious scruff which was how the "in" celebrity males accessorized these days, though he wore it better than most. A battered leather jacket fitted his broad shoulders and gave him a bad-boy-biker look along with worn jeans that hugged his lean hips and muscular thighs. He looked like the guy next door—the good-looking guy next door.

Even if he didn't live on the other side of the country, their paths would never cross because they didn't travel in the same social circles. He had no reason to remember the unremarkable nobody who ran the hospital gift shop. She'd lived in Walnut River for over six years and had never laid eyes on him until his father's funeral.

"I wouldn't expect you to remember me," she said.

"Then you'd be wrong, Mrs. Albright. About remembering you, I mean."

His smile was friendly and attractive and she felt it go straight through her even as she wanted to ask how that bedside manner was working for him. But she had to give him points for showing up.

"Thank you for coming," she said again.

"You sound surprised." The smile disappeared.

"Ella said you were at the airport in New York on your way back to California. I just— I was afraid— Walnut River is so far out of your way that I wasn't sure you'd come."

Boy, was she wrong. But it didn't make sense in her frame of reference. On the spur of the moment a successful, busy plastic surgeon came all this way to see a patient he didn't know? And so fast. Although it felt like a lifetime, the accident was only a few hours ago.

"As it happens, I was in New York for a plastics symposium when my sister called. I came as quickly as I could."

"Out of character for you—" She couldn't believe she'd said that out loud. The words popped out of her mouth before she could stop them. It had been the worst few hours of her life and she was taking it out on him. "Scratch that. How incredibly ungrateful that sounds. I apologize. I'm not at my best right now."

"Forget it," he said, but shadows crept into his eyes. "I understand you work here at the hospital but can't—" He stopped and didn't say whatever it was he'd been about to, but something suspiciously like pity crept into his eyes. "Walnut River isn't that far out of my way and Ella said your daughter's facial injuries are pretty serious."

Tears welled in her eyes again and she turned away, embarrassed by the show of weakness. When he put a comforting hand on her shoulder, the urge to give in to her fear and grief swamped her. With an effort, she pulled herself together and faced him again. She might be the nobody who ran the gift shop but if that connection was what got him here it was one more reason to be grateful for it.

She looked at the half of her daughter's face that she could see and noted the pale skin on Janie's normally healthy pink cheek. "She's been sleeping off and on since the accident."

"That's a combination of shock and medication to keep her comfortable," he explained.

"They told me."

The staff had done an excellent job of keeping her informed. They were her friends as well as coworkers and if not for them, she wasn't sure this wouldn't have broken her.

He walked around to the other side of the bed and very gently pulled away the strips of paper tape loosely holding the gauze over Janie's cheek and ear. "I just got here and wanted to introduce myself and have a quick look at the patient—"

"Janie," she said. "My daughter's name is Jane Josephine Albright. Everyone calls her Janie."

"Janie." He met her gaze, then looked down and continued his examination. "She's a beautiful child."

"Yes, she is—" Courtney stopped, choked up because she wanted to say *was*.

She'd known it was bad or he wouldn't be here.

Courtney remembered very little about the accident and nothing about the helicopter flight that airlifted her and Janie to Walnut River General Hospital. She'd come around and remembered being X-rayed and having her wrist immobilized. The E.R. doctor had ordered CT scans for Janie, then they'd cleaned her up, covered her face and called in a specialist.

No one had pushed Courtney to look and she didn't really want to see. If that made her a coward, so be it. But she didn't think she could bear it, knowing what she'd done to her own child. If she could have her choice of days to do over, today would be at the top of a very long list.

She'd been taking Janie out to an early breakfast before work and school. It was a rare treat because she couldn't afford meals out but Janie had been named student of the month and they'd planned to celebrate. Courtney's gut had told her it wasn't a good idea. The weather was bad. What was that saying? March came in like a lion, out like a lamb? It was true. And she'd worried about the roads being safe.

She should have listened to her gut. She could try and pin this on Mother Nature or God, but the fact was, there was no one else to blame for a single-car rollover accident.

She knew part of her was always trying to make up for the

fact that Janie didn't have a dad. It didn't matter that if he'd lived, Joe wouldn't have been a very good parent. All Janie knew was that her father was gone forever.

Courtney was the mom and trying so very hard to be a good one. Trying *not* to be like her own mother. A powerful wave of guilt washed over her. Her mother had walked out, which was unforgivable, but Courtney had never ended up in a hospital intensive care unit. So which one of them was the worst mother ever? Janie *was* a beautiful child, but she might be scarred for life—and it was all Courtney's fault.

The doctor replaced the gauze and brushed Janie's blond hair off her forehead in a surprising and unexpectedly tender gesture. He met her gaze. "I'm going to look at her chart."

"Is she going to be all right?"

"Her condition is serious, but her injuries aren't life-threatening."

"They already told me that. I want to know if her face is going to be all right."

"I need to evaluate all her test results."

"What aren't you telling me, Dr. Wilder?"

"Please call me David."

She'd call him the devil himself if it would help Janie. She'd call him anything he wanted if he would simply tell her the truth. "David, what are you keeping from me?"

He glanced at Janie and sympathy slid into his vivid blue eyes. "The injuries to her cheek, eye and nose are severe, but I can only see the soft tissue. I need information about muscles, nerves and bone involvement before I can evaluate the extent of the damage. Until I see everything, I can't tell you what kind of outcome you can expect."

"Okay." That made sense. If the little patient in the big bed were anyone other than her child, she'd have realized that without him telling her. It's true what they said about losing objectivity when it concerned someone you loved. "But when you have answers, I want you to tell me everything. The whole truth."

"You have my word, Mrs. Albright."

"Call me Courtney."

He nodded, then walked out. She felt inexplicably alone, which was weird since she hadn't expected him actually to show up at all. Why would he go out of his way? Unless there was something in it for him. She was probably the most un-grateful woman on the planet for thinking such thoughts. But not listening to her gut had cost her in the past and she'd paid a high price today for another lesson.

She didn't have to like the situation, but in her circumstances she had very little choice but to go along with it. The old children's rhyme Humpty Dumpty kept going through her mind.

All the king's horses and all the king's men couldn't put Humpty Dumpty back together again—but none of them were a mom.

David would rather be anywhere but Walnut River, and the feeling wasn't about the CT films he was studying on the viewer. Although it would require a great deal of work, he could repair Janie Albright's face and she would grow up to be as beautiful as her mother. Courtney.

He hadn't known her name until today, but he remembered seeing her the day they'd buried his father. She'd been the single bright spot in his dark void of what-ifs and self-reproach. With her blond hair blowing in the frigid wind, she'd been like a beacon in the sea of pitch black. Her warm brown eyes had been full of sympathy and sadness and he had wondered why she looked that way.

What was her relationship with his father? Why did she mourn so deeply for the man David had disappointed so many years before? More than once since that day he'd recalled her all-American beauty that included a matching set of dimples. His patients who were searching for physical perfection would pay a lot of money to duplicate her looks.

From what Ella had said, Courtney didn't have a lot of money. That meant she needed him. And that made him wary. It wouldn't have if he hadn't been instantly and intensely attracted. But he'd learned a long time ago that intense feelings for a beautiful woman could make a man do stupid things. Life-altering things.

Still, she wasn't the reason he didn't want to be here. That was all about a past filled with mistakes and regrets. It was all about the things he'd done wrong and could never make right. His father was dead and he could never get back time with him or the relationship he'd lost.

At the airport when he'd talked to Ella, his initial reaction had been to plead schedule conflicts that prevented him from coming here. The truth was, he wasn't due back in his Beverly Hills office for several days. The other doctors in the practice would pick up the slack for him. When he'd intended to say no, the word *yes* came out of his mouth. Before she'd hung up, Ella said since he'd be in town Peter would be expecting him at a cocktail party following the rededication of the hospital library in honor of their father. And so it began…

But there was a pressing problem. How was he going to tell a worried young mother that her daughter's damaged face needed extensive work if she was ever going to look normal again?

David pulled Janie's films from the viewer and clicked off the light. After looking through the chart, he walked down the hall and into ICU where he saw Courtney holding her daughter's hand. The little girl was awake and when she saw him, she tensed.

"Mommy—"

Courtney glanced over her shoulder. Like mother, like daughter. She tensed, too. But he had a feeling her fear wasn't all about what he had to tell her. On some level it was personal. Instinctive. He wasn't sure how he knew that, but he'd bet his favorite stethoscope it was true.

Her arm immobilized in a dark-blue sling, she looked back at her daughter. "Sweetie, this is Dr. Wilder. He's come a long way to look at you and tell us what to do to make you better."

David walked over to the bed and smiled down at his patient. "Hi, beautiful."

Janie studied him with her one good eye. It was blue. "Hi."

Underneath the bandage he knew her shattered cheekbone was dragging down her other eye and there was damage to the eyelid. The long gash on her chin and the injury to her ear were the least of the problems and the easiest to fix. There was a six-hour post-trauma window during which repair work could be done without debriding in surgery to avoid infection. It was simplest for the patient and the clock was ticking.

"If I take your mom away for a few minutes will you be all right?" he asked her.

She glanced apprehensively at her mother, then back at him and her mouth trembled. "Why does Mommy have to go with you? Are you gonna fix the bump on her head?"

David knew the injury didn't need his intervention and would heal nicely on its own. Courtney's face would be as flawless as the first time he'd seen her. The fact that she'd refused anything besides basic medical attention in order to remain at her daughter's side showed selflessness and character and a beauty on the inside where it counted most.

He smiled at Janie. "Your mom will be fine without my help. But I need to talk to her for just a couple of minutes."

"'Bout me?"

"Yes," he answered.

"'Bout my face?" Janie asked, a tear sliding down her good cheek. "Mommy said my arm is broken. Is my face broken too?"

Something shifted and stretched in his chest and the feeling made him acutely uncomfortable. A doctor wasn't supposed to become personally involved with a patient, but some had a way of sneaking through his defenses. Janie Albright could easily be one of them.

"Did your mom tell you that Dr. Ella fixed your arm and that's why it's in a cast?" When she nodded, he said, "It's going to be good as new." He chose his words carefully. "There are doctors who can make your face good as new."

"Really?" Courtney asked, hope chasing the wariness from her eyes.

"Really." He looked at the little girl. "And I need to tell your mom all about that, but it's pretty boring. Is it okay with you if we go over there?" he asked, pointing to a spot just inside the door. "You can still see her and we'll be right here if you need anything. How would that be?"

"Okay, I guess," Janie said uncertainly.

"Do you hurt anywhere?" he asked.

"A little." She glanced at the cast on her wrist. "My arm."

"They gave her something for pain a few minutes ago," Courtney told him.

He nodded. "Give it a few minutes, kiddo. You'll feel better. I promise."

"Okay," Janie said.

David moved away from the bed and Courtney followed, cradling her injured arm.

"You promised to tell me like it is," she reminded him, as if she didn't believe he would keep his word.

"And I have every intention of doing that."

She nodded and winced at the movement. "Okay. How bad is her face? Will she really be all right?"

"Yes," he said firmly. "Before I get specific you need to know that she will look normal again."

"Thank God," she said, breathing a sigh of relief.

"But it's going to take work."

Instantly, worry snapped back into place. "Please, explain."

"The damage needs to be repaired in two phases. There's a long deep gash in her chin and her ear needs repair. Also a nick near her eye. With facial trauma we like to suture the damage within six hours of the initial injury or the repairs need to be done in surgery."

Courtney glanced at the clock. "Then there's still time."

"Yes," he agreed. "The second part comes later. Her cheekbone is shattered and the right side of her face needs to be realigned."

Her mouth trembled, and she caught her top lip between her teeth, composing herself as if by sheer force of will. "Go on."

"Instead of trying to piece together the bone fragments, it's my opinion that she'll have a better outcome with an implant."

Courtney considered that for a moment. "She's only six. She's still growing. Will she need more surgery in the future?"

"Possibly. But let's take it one step at a time. And the first step is repairing the superficial damage. Since I'm here, I'll take care of that."

"I don't mean to sound mercenary, especially with my daughter's welfare in question," she said. Her chin lifted a notch as if fierce pride was in major conflict with her survival instincts. "And I'm grateful that you were able to examine her, but it would be best for Janie to have a doctor who's covered under my insurance plan here at work."

"They can do it," he agreed. "But without a specialist's training, the results won't be as favorable. If you want the best possible outcome for Janie, a plastics guy is the way to go. My brother has extended me temporary privileges here at Walnut River General."

"Does that mean my health insurance would cover your services?"

"No." But he was here and this child needed his help now. "But I'm the best man for the job, and there won't be a charge."

She stiffened. "Charity?"

"Your independent streak is showing. I just want to help Janie."

A range of expressions crossed her face, all the way from wariness to resignation. She sighed and said, "Thank you."

"Don't mention it."

She looked fragile, vulnerable and more worried and desperate with every word that came out of his mouth. "How long until phase two?" She took a deep breath. "The implant?"

"After the swelling goes down. My best guess is about three to four weeks."

"Tell me it's not more complicated than phase one," she said.

He met her gaze head-on. "She's going to need surgery."

"That's complicated."

"And someone who specializes in reconstructive surgery," he confirmed.

"Okay. Three to four weeks." She nodded and glanced at her daughter, clearly trying to process the information as rationally as possible. "Then I'll have time to check out my health-care coverage."

David knew for a fact that there wasn't a doctor in Walnut River who could do the procedure. "I'd be happy to recommend someone good who's as close to Walnut River as possible."

"So there could be more out-of-pocket expenses," she said absently, almost as if she were thinking out loud.

"It's possible." Ella had told him she was a single mother. That probably meant divorced. He wished he could be indifferent to the fact that she was unattached but there was a part of him that couldn't seem to work up a proper level of regret. Still, divorced parents came together for their children. "Surely Janie's father will help—"

"Hardly." Unexpected bitterness filled Courtney's gaze. "Her father was a soldier."

Too late now to wish he'd paid more attention when his sister had told him about a single mom who had big trouble. "Was?"

"He died in Iraq. Unfortunately he wasn't as conscientious about military dependent's benefits as he should have been."

"I'm sorry."

About that and so much more. He was an idiot. An idiot who made assumptions. An idiot who felt himself being sucked in by big brown eyes and a pair of dimples that wouldn't quit. Courtney Albright desperately needed his help.

The last time he'd become involved with a desperate woman it had cost him everything.

Chapter Two

Courtney held her little girl's small hand while they both watched David snap on his latex gloves, then inspect the metal tray full of medical tools beside him. She was pretty sure her own eyes were as wide as her daughter's and the fear factor was up there for both of them. If only she was the one facing the procedure. That would have been so much easier than watching Janie go through it. And that wasn't the end of the ordeal. There was still a surgery, but she couldn't deal with that now. One trauma at a time.

David had changed into blue scrubs and it was disconcerting that he looked just as good as he had in his jeans and leather jacket. How stupid was she for even thinking that?

"Okay, beautiful, are you ready?" David asked.

She assumed he meant Janie since he was looking at her. "Do you have any questions, peanut?" Courtney questioned.

"Is it gonna hurt?" Her mouth trembled as she looked at him.

He looked at Janie. "I'm going to give you some medicine so it won't hurt. A small pinch and then nothing."

"Promise?"

"Yes."

"What else is gonna happen?"

"I won't lie to you, Janie." David met her gaze. "I'm going to tell you exactly what's going on."

"No medical doublespeak requiring a translator?" Courtney asked.

"Honesty is always the best policy." He must have seen the skepticism in her eyes because he added, "Especially with children. They always know when something's not right. It's my goal to keep her calm. If she's not prepared for this she's going to get agitated. Agitation is quickly followed by restlessness, then tension and stress. None of that is helpful."

That made sense. "I see your point."

He nodded, then focused on the child. "You're going to feel a little pulling. Do you think you can be very still for me? More still than any other six-year-old girl ever?" When Janie nodded solemnly, he smiled. "Okay. Let's do this."

Courtney squeezed her daughter's fingers while David picked up a swab and dabbed it over the area. He'd already explained that it was a topical anesthetic to take the edge off the injection that would numb her for the procedure. Now was where she did her mom thing. She needed to distract Janie while David worked.

"I think a six-year-old who can be more still than anyone ever deserves a special prize," she said.

"What?" Janie asked, her attention snagged as hoped for.

"It's got to be pretty special. What's the most special thing you can think of?"

"What about ice cream?" David suggested.

"I like vanilla ice cream," Janie said. "Milkshakes are best. But I think a toy would be good, too."

"What toy?" Courtney asked.

"Maybe a doll. With a stroller."

"Okay, Janie. It's time to hold still for me. Then we can get serious about that doll-and-stroller thing."

Janie tensed and whimpered when he did the injections but she barely moved a muscle.

Several moments later he announced, "All finished with that part. And it's the worst. I promise. Now we wait for the medicine to do its work."

"Do I win the prize?" Janie wanted to know.

"Hands down," he agreed.

"Are you finished?"

He shook his head. "I still have a little more to do."

"What?" Janie asked. She glanced at the tray of instruments beside him. "Where's the needle?"

Courtney winced and felt David's gaze on her. "I think everything the doctor is going to use is wrapped up there on the tray."

"Why?"

"To keep them sterile," David explained. "To keep the germs off. Did you ever have a scratch or scrape that got infected?"

The little girl pressed her lips together. "One time. It got really red and hurt. Mommy had to pour this stuff on—"

"Hydrogen peroxide," Courtney said when Janie glanced at her for clarification.

"Then she put on cream and I got a Band-Aid."

"Your mom did just the right thing," David said.

Courtney felt the power of his praise course through her but that made no sense. Why should it make any difference to her whether or not he approved? And yet it did. How irritating was that? The good news was that Janie had been successfully distracted.

"You'll heal faster if these cuts don't get any germs in them," he explained.

"You have to sew up my boo-boo?" she asked.

He thought for a moment. "I have to pull the edges together so it heals neatly."

"Are you gonna use a big needle? Like the one my mommy uses to fix my jeans?"

His face was intensely serious as he answered the question. "I'm not sure what your mom uses for that," he said, "but for what I'm going to do we need everything as small as possible."

"'Cuz I'm small?"

Courtney's throat tightened with emotion. Her child was too small to go through this, she thought. She knew she should say something, but couldn't get anything past the lump in her throat. Some pillar of strength she was.

David's sharp-eyed gaze seemed to pick up on her state of mind. "Janie, even if you were as big as Shrek I would use very tiny stuff."

"How come?"

"Because tiny stuff will make the scar almost invisible."

"So that stuff is magic?"

"In the right hands it is."

Courtney looked at his long, elegant gloved fingers. "Are your hands magic?"

"Yes." He smiled.

His tone wasn't arrogant, just matter-of-fact. There was nothing even remotely sensual or suggestive in his response or the way he looked at her, but Courtney felt that smile dance over her skin and touch her everywhere. She swore she felt tingles and considering her opinion of this man, he wielded some kind of powerful magic.

"You said 'almost' invisible. That means a little bit visible," she said, glancing at Janie.

"It does." He glanced at Janie, too, gauging her reaction. "Believe it or not, there's some good news."

"I could sure use some of that," Courtney answered, and she'd never meant anything more in her entire life.

With a gloved finger, he pointed to the long gash on her chin. "Because this is on the jawline, it will be practically unnoticeable under her chin. Her ear, while exceptionally lovely and delicate, has creases and folds."

"Like Mr. Potato Head?" Janie asked.

David laughed. "You're much prettier than he is. But here's the thing, ears have lots of places to hide the sutures. And so does your eye—a natural fold between your eyelid and brow bone. It's a matter of using what nature gave you for camouflage. All of that makes my job easier."

Courtney was relieved to hear that, but wondered if he took the easy way out in his personal life, too. It was as if he was all about how things appeared on the outside. He'd come home for his mother's funeral, then his father's. But nothing in between. She'd known James Wilder pretty well. For some reason the man had taken an interest in her and Janie and his passing left a big hole in her life. But while his father was still alive, David never came to visit. It wasn't a stretch to conclude that he didn't take after the elder Dr. Wilder who'd cared more about the inside of people than the outside.

"Okay, Janie, I'm going to start. Are you ready to hold still again?"

"You don't need a nurse?" Courtney asked.

He shook his head. "I'm used to working alone, and they're busy."

"Is it okay if I shut my eyes?" Janie said.

"If you want."

Courtney wished she could shut her eyes too, but from where she was sitting in the chair, she couldn't really see much anyway. Just the slow, methodical way his elegant hands moved. The suture material was so fine it was barely visible and he held it with forceps. Between the pain medication she'd received and being physically drained from what she'd been through, Janie actually drifted off while David worked.

He might not be much like his father, but he was really good with her daughter. It seemed natural, something she wouldn't have expected. "Where did you learn to get along with kids?"

His gaze met hers briefly. "I was one once."

So was she. About a million years ago. On second thought, she didn't actually remember being a kid. It seemed as if she'd always been the grown-up, handling one crisis after another when her father was too drunk even to take care of himself.

But if David had taken a course in med school on how to charm children, apparently he'd aced it. The man was putting sutures in Janie's chin and she trusted him enough to fall asleep. The ability to do that didn't mesh with what little Courtney knew about him.

"But you're not a kid now," she said. That was the understatement of the century. He was a man who sprinkled sex appeal like fairy dust wherever he went, if tabloid stories linking him to models and actresses were anything to go by. "And you didn't talk down to her."

"Kids know when you do that. They don't like it."

She actually laughed. "That's true."

Who'd have thought anyone could make her laugh under the circumstances? Maybe he was magic. That thought made her uneasy and when she was uneasy it was time to fall back on defenses.

"So why did you agree to look at Janie?" she asked.

He glanced at her. "Because my sister called."

"But you're not helping your sister. Janie and I are total strangers to you." And from what she gathered, his family wasn't too much more to him. Yet he was here because Ella called. By any definition that was a nice thing. Men who did nice things usually wanted something and she wasn't comfortable with that kind of balance sheet.

"Let's just say this is the least I can do for the widow and daughter of a war hero," he said.

Courtney cringed at his words. It was what everyone thought, and it couldn't be further from the truth. The anger welled up and after a day like today she didn't have the emotional reserves to bite her tongue.

"Joining the army wasn't about truth, justice and the American way for Joe. My husband was a lot of things, but noble wasn't one of them."

David's hands stopped moving and he looked at her. "He gave his life for his country. That seems pretty noble to me."

It would have been if his reasons for joining the military hadn't been about getting away from his wife and baby girl. He'd gone because he wanted liberty, but not for his country. For himself. He wanted freedom from domestic restraints so he could play around with women, any woman who wasn't his wife.

As quickly as the rage reared up, it let her down. She was so tired. Tired of being angry about something she couldn't change. Mostly she was just tired. And sore. It felt as if every muscle ached and her body was the percussion section in a marching band. Her head throbbed, then her wrist pounded. And that was her only excuse for revealing relationship failures to the doctor who'd been nice enough to help Janie.

She met his questioning gaze and sighed. "Is it too late to take that back?"

"Pretty much," he confirmed.

She sighed. "Ordinarily I'm not prone to sharing personal information. Especially with someone I don't know. Someone who went out of his way to do a nice thing. I can only plead probable brain damage after hitting my head. How about we pretend I didn't say anything?"

"Okay."

That was too easy. Or maybe not. He probably didn't want to hear her tragic story any more than she wanted to tell it. When his good deed was done, he'd be out of here. And it couldn't be too soon for her. The man did things to her. He'd surprised her when he was so good with Janie. It surprised her when he'd picked up the slack in the support department when she was feeling about as strong as a fettuccine noodle. She didn't like surprises.

They were never good.

David rolled his disposable gloves off and dropped them on the tray beside him, then studied his work. He'd made the sutures as tiny as humanly possible and knew that the stubborn little chin would heal nicely. When he noted Courtney's pale face he figured it best not to make her study the finished product.

But he couldn't resist saying, "Not bad."

"Humble, aren't you?" Edgy sarcasm laced the words, but he had a feeling that spirit was the only reason she was still on her feet.

He decided to help her out. "Haven't you heard? Arrogance is a prerequisite for doctors."

"I've heard that. But I haven't seen it up close and personal until now."

He vaguely remembered Ella saying Courtney was a hospital employee, but a bad connection while he was in the airport had prevented him hearing in what capacity. Because of that call, he was here instead of on a plane to L.A.

When he looked at Courtney's mouth, his wish that he were on a plane to anywhere took hold. Her lips took up forty-five percent of her face—a slight exaggeration, but if she didn't have the sexiest mouth he'd ever seen, he'd turn in his forceps and start making house calls.

"You *do* work here at the hospital," he clarified.

"I manage the gift shop."

"So you don't work directly with doctors?"

"No."

She met his gaze and didn't look away, but he'd swear her self-respect took a hit. Something in her eyes dimmed, some inner spark that was struggling to burst into flame all but sputtered and went out. He wasn't sure what he'd said, but he wanted to fix it, even though he'd tried fixing things for a woman once and it hadn't gone well.

"You're lucky you don't work with doctors," he said. "There's a whole needing-to-be-right, needing-to-be-worshipped thing that can get pretty annoying."

"With so many doctors in your family, that must be an interesting dynamic."

It probably would be if he'd spent any significant time with them. But he hadn't. Not since his father had told him he couldn't stand the sight of him. David had lashed out, defended actions that really had no defense. But he'd been in love and the woman who'd captured his heart had stolen his soul. It wasn't long before he found out she'd been using his feelings for her to make him a puppet who jumped when she yanked his strings.

He'd lost the person he cared about most because of her and no matter what he did, there didn't seem to be any way to fill up the void.

His thoughts hadn't taken this pathetic a turn for a long time and when he looked at Courtney's full lips, it occurred to him that the sooner he got out of Walnut River the better.

And he would. But right now Janie needed a sterile dressing on her chin. He could have called a nurse to do it, but after the arrogance discussion, he figured it wouldn't hurt to do it himself. Which wasn't a problem. He'd had a lot of practice on his overseas trips. Arrogance had no place in a Nicaraguan jungle or an African desert.

After cutting several strips of paper tape, he unwrapped a nonstick pad and secured it to the little girl's determined chin. It crossed his mind that she'd inherited that from her mother, along with her dimples. At some point he was going to have to break the news to Courtney that her daughter wouldn't ever again have a matched set. So far that detail hadn't come up, most likely because she'd been more worried about the big picture. And for now that was more important.

When he saw Courtney watching him intently, he said, "She's going to be sore for a while. Chewing will probably cause her some discomfort and she may not want to eat, but she has to keep her strength up. Here in the hospital they'll give her soft foods, but when you take her home, she probably won't want a steak for awhile."

"Okay. And, for the record, she doesn't really like steak."

"But you get my drift." He gently smoothed the edges of the tape. "These sutures should be checked in a day or two and will probably need to come out in about a week. For facial trauma, we don't like to leave them in too long."

"Why not?"

"Too long can be worse than not long enough. If soft tissue heals around the suture, it's too hard to remove and can cause pulling. Not what we want."

"Okay."

"In plastics, one of the first things you learn is that the tenderest tissue needs the gentlest touch."

Courtney's battered face was clear evidence that fate hadn't dealt especially gently with her today. But it was the shadows in her eyes that made him wonder about her past, the personal stuff she'd let slip. Patients didn't always tell the truth and doctors learned to read between the lines. It seemed likely that Courtney was bruised and tender on the inside and needed a very soft touch. From someone besides him.

David walked around the bed and looked down at Courtney. "That's all we can do for now. She's resting comfortably. It's time you took care of yourself."

"I'm fine."

"That's a nasty bump on your head."

"That's all it is. Nothing showed up on the CT scan."

"What about your wrist?"

"Dr. Wilder—" She stopped as one corner of her mouth curved up. "Your sister looked at the X-rays and said it might need surgery but she couldn't be sure until the swelling goes down. So I don't have an appointment for the O.R. tonight."

Was that a hint? Not likely if the semi-hostile looks she'd lobbed at him were anything to go by. "And no hot date?"

"Oh, please," she said wryly. "I've sworn off men."

"And you're sharing that only because of that bump on your head?"

"That's my story and I'm sticking to it." She pointed to the nasty-looking contusion. "However bad you think it looks on the outside, it's way worse on the inside."

She meant her body, but he'd been talking about her spirit. Must be something about being back in Walnut River, in the hospital his father had nurtured into the fine facility it was today. Something was turning his thoughts to a dark, introspective place and he didn't much like going there. It was pointless to spend any energy on things he couldn't change. Practical considerations were much less complicated. Like what his sister, Ella, had decided about Courtney.

"I'll ask Ella to give you something for the pain," he suggested.

"No. I'm fine. Over-the-counter pain meds are taking the edge off. Anything stronger will make me sleepy and I need to keep as clear a head as I can. For Janie."

"She's being well cared for. Maybe you should take the doctor's advice and be admitted to the hospital."

"Not even on a bet."

"Why?"

"Because I don't need to take up a bed."

"Why are you fighting it? You have insurance—"

"There's a deductible," she interrupted. "And I'm okay. Besides, I can't take care of Janie from a hospital bed."

"You can't take care of Janie at all if you don't take care of yourself first. If you won't take the doctor's advice, at least go home and get some rest."

"I don't have a car. It's a little banged up, too. And even if I did, Ella said I probably shouldn't drive for a couple of days."

David folded his arms over his chest as he stared down at her. "So you embrace the orders you like and scrap everything else."

"Pretty much."

"I'll take you home," he said, then cursed himself for knuckling to the appeal of a needy woman.

"Thanks, but I can't leave. Janie and I appreciate everything you did, David. Thank you for coming."

That was a dismissal if he'd ever heard one. She was telling him to go, that his work here was done. That she could take it from here. He *should* go, and he planned to…until he made the mistake of looking at her, sitting in a chair and holding her sleeping child's hand. By sheer strength of will she was going to sit here. Probably all night. He stared for several moments at her delicate profile, the strain, the bruises, the pride, the guts and he couldn't just walk out.

One more time. "Courtney, your body has been through a trauma, too. Rest is the best thing—" He stopped when she shot him a look—fiercely female and protective.

"How can I rest when my baby is in the hospital? What if she wakes up and gets scared? What if she needs me? It's my fault she's here in the first place. I have to live with that, but I could never live with myself if I left her here all alone." She shook her head with a vehemence that had to hurt. "I'm not going anywhere. Again, thanks for everything. Good night, David."

He sat down in the chair beside hers and noticed her staring. "What?"

"That's what I'd like to know." Courtney frowned. "What are you doing?"

"Probably the reason Ella wanted you admitted was for observation. To make sure you're okay. Consider yourself observed on an outpatient basis."

"Oh, for Pete's sake. That's silly. You should go. I'm fine. And if I'm not, the nurses are in and out. Help is right here."

"You can't stay here all night. Sooner or later they're going to throw you out."

"I'm willing to risk it."

"Okay." He stretched out his legs and rested his hands on his abdomen. He didn't need to be at Peter's cocktail party for a while. "I'll keep you company."

Courtney looked puzzled. "I don't understand why you're doing this."

That made two of them. "Does it matter?"

"It kind of does in my world." She stared at him. "I haven't known many people who gave to others without having a personal agenda. Your father was one."

"What did he give you?"

"My job in the gift shop for one thing. I needed it badly and somehow he knew that. He sort of took Janie and me under his wing and watched out for us. Never once did he ask for anything in return."

But *he'd* been on the receiving end of his father's dark side. Everybody had one, even James Wilder.

"Hell of a guy," David said.

"That he was. You look a lot like him," Courtney observed.

"Is that a compliment?"

"Maybe. Mostly just stating a fact. But you're very different from him."

"Another fact?"

"Just an observation."

"Based on what?" he asked.

"Based on the fact that your father went out of his way to befriend a stranger."

"And?"

"What makes you think there's an 'and'?"

"Don't ever try to bluff in a poker game, Court. Your feelings are all over your face," he said. He should know. Faces were his bread and butter.

"Okay. Remember you asked. I can't imagine your father going long periods of time without visiting his family."

"Unless they screwed with his moral code," David snapped. She was right. He shouldn't have asked.

"So your father disapproved of something you did?" she guessed.

His father had disapproved of almost everything he did. "Didn't he tell you I was Walnut River's resident bad boy?"

"Really?"

He nodded. "Every time I rode my motorcycle through town people said there goes that Wilder boy, living up to his name again." When he looked over at her she was smiling, which somehow took the sting out of the memories.

"You had a motorcycle?"

"I paid for it myself."

"So you and your father had issues?" she asked.

"My father said I needed my head examined and if I insisted on riding the bike it was only a question of time until it happened."

"Want to talk about the deeper issues?" she asked.

"You want to talk about your husband?" he shot back.

"Not especially."

"Me either," he agreed.

She was quiet for several moments before saying, "It just seems to me that whatever you did must have been pretty bad to cut yourself off from family."

"So you're an expert on family matters?"

"Hardly." She shook her head. "I never had one, which is why it strikes me as so incredibly sad that you'd ignore a perfectly good one."

"Have you ever heard that saying—don't judge someone until you've walked a mile in their shoes?"

"Yes. And I stand by what I said."

"Meaning you don't think much of me."

"Look, I don't mean to be an ungrateful witch. And my opinion is worth exactly what you paid for it—"

"But?"

"I knew your father and the distance between you must have hurt him a lot."

"Distance goes both ways," he shot back, knowing it was lame and childish.

But the anger was gone as quickly as it ignited. Not reaching out was one more transgression in a long list. David had always thought there would be time to make things right. Even if Courtney had a point, which he wasn't saying she did, there was no way to fix it now. His father was dead and any chance of rectifying the past had died with him.

Speaking of death, she was a widow and obviously understood losing someone—even someone she had issues with. But the man had died in service to his country. Either her standards were a tad high or she had just cause. He found himself curious when he didn't want to be interested in anything about Courtney Albright.

What he'd done had violated more than his father's moral code. And he'd done it because he was desperately in love with a woman who needed him. He'd thought they loved enough to do anything for each other. But that woman was only thinking about herself when she used him. He had a hunch Courtney was in desperate need, which made trusting her a no-brainer. But he couldn't resist wanting to help her either. Over time he'd learned how to help without getting emotionally involved, but that was a dangerous slope and already his hold was slipping.

That was why he needed to get on a plane back to L.A. as soon as possible.

Chapter Three

In the bathroom down the hall from the pediatric ICU, Courtney pulled on the blue scrubs the nurses had found for her and tugged the waistband tight. She wouldn't win any fashion awards, but at least they were clean. It felt good to wash the accident off. Then she glanced in the mirror and nearly shrieked.

Her hair was drying naturally and without a blow dryer the effect wasn't pretty. There were bruises on her forehead and the ones on her cheekbone could be an extension of the dark circles under her eyes, a by-product of not sleeping the night before. Catnaps in the chair beside Janie's bed didn't count, but there was no way she would abandon her child. It had taken a lot of persuasion and the threat of physical intervention for the nurses to talk her into leaving long enough to clean up.

As she walked down the hall alone, preparing to deal with whatever came along today, she remembered how good David's company had felt until he'd excused himself for a cocktail party hosted by his brother Peter following the rededication of the hospital library to their father. But that was yesterday. Today was situation normal—her and Janie against the world.

When she walked into her daughter's room, she stopped short. Correction: Janie wasn't alone. David was there, looking far too good in his worn jeans and black body-hugging T-shirt. It made him look every inch the bad boy he'd said he used to be. The leather jacket was draped across the back of the chair she'd slept in last night.

Her heart stuttered, sputtered, then shifted into high gear as a wave of warmth swelled through her and settled in her cheeks. He looked like a movie star and she looked like a really unfortunate "before" picture. Courtney knew it was bad to care about how she looked to him and worse to be so ridiculously happy that he was here. Bad to worse didn't change the fact that both were true.

Her daughter waved and pointed to the biggie-sized cup bearing the logo from Buns 'n' Burgers that he was holding.

"I'm so happy to see you eating something." She walked over to the bed and kissed Janie's forehead then checked out the contents of the cup. All evidence pointed to the fact that it was a vanilla milkshake. "Wow, sweetie, your favorite. Where did you get that?"

"Buns 'n' Burgers," David said.

She slid him a wry look. "Let me rephrase. Buns 'n' Burgers isn't a delivery kind of place. How did it get here? Did one of the nurses bring it?"

Janie shook her head and pointed to David.

He shrugged. "When I called for a progress report, her nurse said she wasn't eating. So I took the liberty—"

"It wasn't necessary for you to go out of your way," she said. "I could have gotten her one here at the hospital."

"Rumor has it that Buns 'n' Burgers is her favorite place. Besides, I wanted to see if the food is as good as I remembered," he explained.

"And?" Courtney asked.

"I've been all over the world and never tasted better."

"And you remembered that vanilla milkshakes are her favorite."

Janie nodded and rubbed her tummy.

Courtney frowned. "Is something wrong? You haven't said anything, kiddo."

"She told me that it feels weird on her chin when she talks. So I suggested she not talk." David folded his arms over his chest, drawing her attention to his wide shoulders and flat abdomen.

As soon as the word *hot* popped into her head, Courtney turned back to her daughter. The little girl pointed to her arm, which was in a sling.

"She wants to know if your wrist hurts," David said.

"I got that." Amused, Courtney looked back at him. "But since when did you learn to interpret sign language from a six-year-old girl?"

"You've heard of a horse whisperer," he said.

"Yes. And you're what? A babe whisperer?" She couldn't resist the zinger or hold back a smile.

"Exactly," he said, not without smugness. "I understand women from six to sixty."

"Word on the street is that you concentrate your powers of persuasion in the twenty-to-thirty range."

"Do you always believe everything you hear?"

"Yeah," she said, nodding. "Pretty much."

Janie tapped David's arm and he lifted the cup closer to her mouth. She made a noisy job of finishing every last drop of her milkshake, then reclined in the bed with a satisfied sigh. She was on the mend, thanks to David. But Courtney hadn't expected to see him again.

She looked up at him. "I thought you'd be on the first plane back to L.A."

"I wanted to check in on Janie. Make sure everything's okay this morning."

And bring her favorite food to coax her to eat. Courtney didn't trust this heroic act and wondered what he was after.

"And?" she asked.

He grinned. "I'm happy to say the stitches look good and there's no sign of infection."

"If every part of my body didn't hurt, I'd be doing the dance of joy," she said.

"Can I have a rain check?" Amusement was another good look for him.

They stared at each other for several moments and the pulse at the base of her throat began to flutter. "So," she said, dragging out the word slightly, "the airport is probably your next stop after you leave here?"

His expression was bemused. "Since I'm here, I thought a short visit would be nice."

"Family before facelifts?" As soon as the words were out, she put her hand over her mouth.

"Shoots and scores," he said, one eyebrow lifting.

"David, I—" She shook her head and felt like the world's biggest jerk. "I'm not sure why you bring out my snarky side—"

"So it's my fault?" His mouth twitched with amusement. "If I were a shrink," he said, "I'd have a field day with how you can't take responsibility for your sarcastic streak."

"I'm pretty tired." She blew out a breath. "In my own defense I have to say that spending the night here doesn't reveal my naturally sweet disposition."

"I'll look forward to seeing it."

There was no good way to interpret the cryptic comment so she refused to think about what he meant. "I was teasing and it came out wrong. Your relationship with your family is none of my business."

"True. But since we both seem to be defending ourselves, let me say that my family understands being busy. Medicine is a demanding mistress and everyone but my sister, Anna, is a doctor."

Courtney noticed the slight frown when he mentioned his sister, which was a different—darker—expression from when he'd talked about his other siblings. She wanted to ask, but until she could regain full function of the filter between her brain and her mouth, she figured it was better not to comment.

The fact was that doctors *were* busy. His father had put in long days here at the hospital until he retired. It's where she'd met him after Janie was born. When her husband had moved them to Walnut River—scratch that. He'd dumped her pregnant and alone in this town, then taken off to join the army. Like everyone else, at first she'd thought him noble and patriotic. It wasn't until later that she'd found out his motives were selfish and shallow. Everything he'd done—and what he hadn't done—had cost her. Everything except leaving her here.

She'd grown to love this place and that had started with James Wilder. She knew his son Peter from working here. And recently Dr. Ella Wilder had returned. But Courtney had never met his other sister.

"I don't know Anna," she said.

"Me either," he answered, so softly she wasn't sure she'd heard right. And his frown deepened.

"Mommy, I'm a little bored."

Janie wasn't too uncomfortable to talk. But that wasn't the only reason Courtney felt tears well in her eyes. A lump of emotion jumped from her chest to push against her throat. "I'm so glad," she whispered.

David looked puzzled. "The dance of joy because she's bored?"

"What happened to the 'babe whisperer'?"

"I guess my radar is down. Care to explain?"

"Normally those words are enough to send a mother over the edge. But in this case they're so incredibly normal. After what she's been through, it's dance-of-joy worthy."

"Ah," he said. "Keep in mind that kids are pretty resilient."

She knew he was warning her to keep a stiff upper lip through what was to come, but she couldn't think about that now. She'd take every victory she could get.

"Do you have many patients who are children?" she asked.

"Some," he said mysteriously. But there was something in his eyes, something he wasn't telling.

"Mommy, what am I going to do?"

"I'll turn on the TV," she suggested.

Janie shook her head. "It's all cartoons or baby shows."

"And you're so grown up," David teased. He walked over to his jacket and pulled something out of the pocket. "How about a game of cards?"

"I don't know how to play," Janie said.

"Then I'll teach you."

"Do I hafta hold 'em?" Janie lifted her right arm and showed off her hot-pink wrist cast.

"No." He pulled over the mobile table, then rested his hip on her bed. "You can put your cards in your lap face up. I won't peek."

"Promise?" Janie said.

He made an *X* over his heart. "Promise."

Courtney's heart would have to be three sizes too small not to be moved by his attention and gentle caring. She watched David patiently explain the rules of Old Maid, Go Fish and solitaire. Although one eye was covered in bandages, Janie's good eye sparkled when she looked at David. Her little girl liked the handsome charmer.

Courtney's feelings were far more complicated. She was

attracted to and wary of this man in equal parts. They said patients fell in love with their doctors, but she wasn't sure that held true for mothers of patients. Fortunately she wouldn't have to test the theory.

He had a glamorous life clear across the country, as far removed from the Walnut River lifestyle as you could get. Courtney was both incredibly grateful for what he'd done and extraordinarily relieved that there wasn't a snowball's chance in hell that he'd be staying to tempt her.

It was dark outside when David peeked into Janie's room much later that day. Courtney was sitting exactly where he'd left her earlier and the oversized blue scrubs were a big clue that she'd been there without a break. Over twenty-four hours had passed since the accident. Had she slept properly? Eaten anything? And since when did patient-care protocols extend to the patient's mother? Was she the reason he kept coming back here to check? Because there was nothing further he could do for Janie.

Correction: nothing until her initial injuries healed. By that time he'd be back at his Beverly Hills office. He remembered the way worry had darkened Courtney's eyes when she realized everything would be more financially complicated because the procedure couldn't be done here. Insurance companies could get squirrelly about paying for medical costs that were considered "cosmetic." But this little girl could be disfigured for the rest of her life if the repair wasn't done. He told himself that's why he couldn't get Courtney out of his mind.

She stood by the hospital bed and stretched her good arm over her head, then rolled her shoulders as if everything were stiff. The baggy scrubs didn't hide the fact that she had curves in all the right places. If anything, that made him want to see for himself. A warm twang in his chest startled him and when she glanced in his direction, he thought the sound had found its way out.

"Hi." Her voice reflected the surprised expression in her eyes.

He raised a hand in greeting. "Hi."

"I didn't expect to see you."

"I came back to see my brother." Only half a lie. Peter had gone for the day, but there was no reason to mention that. "How's Janie?"

"Asleep." She took a quick look, then walked over to him. "She was in some discomfort so they gave her something. On top of that I think she's pretty exhausted."

"Sleep is the best thing for her. Is she eating?"

"A little. They're trying to tempt her with burgers, mac and cheese and chocolate puddings. But she said her favorite thing was the milkshake you brought her. That was very nice of you, by the way."

He shrugged. "I'm glad she enjoyed it. Good to know some things don't change—like the food in your favorite hangout."

"Must have been nice to have a hangout," she said wistfully.

The remark made him curious. "Where did you and your friends spend time?"

"Here and there," she said vaguely. "So, how much longer will you be here?"

"You seem awfully anxious to get rid of me," he accused.

"No." The denial was too quick and the look on her face too much like the proverbial deer caught in headlights. "It's just you're a busy doctor and I figured you needed to get back to your patients."

"Janie is my patient, too."

"And you've done everything you can for now. But you're just passing through and we don't want to keep you from—"

He held up his hand. "If it's not nice, you'll hate yourself for saying something snarky."

Her expression was exaggerated innocence. "I was just going to say that all those rich women desperate to smooth out the worry lines in their foreheads need love too."

David couldn't shake the feeling that this was her way of saying "don't let the door hit you in the backside on your way out." Her sincere gratitude for his help was real, no question about that. So there must be another reason she was anxious to get rid of him. Did she feel the sparks between them too? The more she pushed, the greater his inclination to push back, to dig his heels in and see how she reacted. How perverse was that?

"Have you eaten anything today?" he asked, changing the subject.

She blinked. "What?"

"Have you taken a break from this room and had anything to eat?"

"I'm not your patient, David."

"That doesn't mean I'm not concerned about you."

"Don't be. I've been taking care of my daughter and myself for a very long time."

Since her husband died. But he had the feeling it had started even before that and he wanted to know more.

"Have dinner with me," he said.

She glanced over at the bed where Janie was still sleeping soundly. "I can't leave her."

"Do you have a cell phone?"

"I'm not sure that's relevant, but yes," she said.

"If she needs you they can call. You need some fresh air and non-hospital food."

"I'm fine." But her stomach chose that moment to growl. Loudly. She met his gaze and her expression turned sheepish when she knew he'd heard, too.

"Fine, but hungry."

"In spite of what you heard, I don't have much appetite," she protested.

"Look, you can keep throwing out lame excuses, or just suck it up and let me take you to dinner."

"David, I'll just cut to the chase." She suddenly looked drawn and tired. "You're obviously a caring man but you've let things slip. I'm fairly certain that handsome face of yours hides all kinds of demons. The truth is, I just don't need one more challenge in my life."

"Was that a compliment?" he asked.

"Which part?" she said, her forehead furrowing as she thought.

"The handsome part."

A flush crept into her cheeks, welcome color to chase away the paleness. "Must be post-accident loose-tongue syndrome again."

"Must be." He slid his fingertips into the pockets of his jeans. "Would you say yes to dinner if I promise to leave my demons in the car?"

When one corner of her mouth curved up it was clear she was weakening. "Can it be my treat?"

"Okay, as long as we take my car."

She sent him a wry look. "Since I don't have a car at the moment, I have to ask—is that sarcasm, Doctor?"

"I guess I've been hanging out with you too long. But it has to be said that I've learned from the best."

David found himself back at Buns 'n' Burgers on Lexington Avenue for two reasons—it was close to the hospital and in Courtney's budget. They ordered at the counter, got a number for table delivery and he carried their tray to a secluded corner booth.

She slid in with a tired sigh. "I feel so darn guilty."

"Because?" He sat across from her.

"The fresh air feels so good. What kind of mother am I to be enjoying the world outside Walnut River General while my child is there?"

"She's asleep, Court. She doesn't know you're not there. If she needs you, they'll call. Relax and recharge your batteries."

A teenage boy in a yellow Buns 'n' Burgers shirt and matching hat delivered their cheeseburgers and fries, asked if they needed anything else, then left after an automatic, "Enjoy your meal."

With her good hand, Courtney picked up her burger and wolfed it down as though she hadn't eaten in a month. She chewed the last bite and—he was going to hell for this thought—she looked like a woman satisfied by the best sex of her life.

"Good burger?" he asked. Even if he didn't feel the physical evidence, the inane question would have been positive proof that blood flow from his brain had been diverted to points south.

"I'm fairly sure that was the best hamburger I've ever had." She took her time with the fries. "So, tell me more about growing up in Walnut River—specifically about being 'that Wilder boy.'"

"I thought you wanted me to leave my demons in the car."

"Now that I've been fed and watered, I find myself with the strength and curiosity to pull those demons out and take 'em for a spin." She dipped a fry in ketchup, then popped it in her mouth and chewed thoughtfully. "There's something I don't understand. You seemed to have a great childhood. So where did the demons come from?"

So many demons, so little time. One was a father devoted to his work and any time left over had been lavished on an adopted daughter at the expense of everyone else in the family—including his mother.

"Can we just chalk it up to sowing my wild oats?" he asked.

"No." She grinned. "So out with it—any smoking, drinking and general wickedness?"

"You have quite the imagination," he said.

"You're evading the question," she accused, jabbing the air in his direction with a French fry.

He thought back. "There were the usual lectures about grades and living up to my potential. Curfew violations. Typical rebellion. A couple of run-ins with the cops. After all, I was 'that Wilder boy.'"

"Did you really have a motorcycle?"

"Yeah. No pun intended, but it drove my parents nuts."

"I don't blame them," she said. "What were you thinking?"

"Short answer—I wasn't. Teenage boys aren't notoriously rational. It's more about testosterone."

"Just as teenagers?" she teased.

He shook his head. "Not going there. That's a demon not pertinent to this discussion."

"Why not?"

"Because it's your turn."

"For?"

"Childhood confessions." The shadows in her expression took him by surprise. Suddenly the spark flickered and went out. He was torn between really wanting to know about her and needing to put the smile back on her face. "What is it, Courtney?"

"You don't really want to hear the sad details."

"You're wrong."

"You're leaving."

"I'm here now."

She hesitated for several moments, then said, "My mother skipped out on my dad and me when I was Janie's age. No note. No good-bye. Just one day when I woke up she was gone."

She was so obviously deeply committed to her child and

he had instinctively assumed the fruit didn't fall far from the tree. For some reason, he hadn't expected that. "I don't know what to say."

"You could say it sucked. Because it did. I never saw her again."

"How did your dad take it?"

She laughed but it was the saddest sound he'd ever heard. "I can't say he didn't drink before she walked out. But I can tell you with absolute certainty that he was rarely sober after. Trauma tends to highlight things like that."

"Courtney—"

"Don't." She held up her hand. "I hate hearing clichés and despise being one even more. But in this case it's the God's honest truth. I'm walking, talking, *surviving* proof that what doesn't kill you definitely makes you stronger."

"So you never really got to be a kid."

She looked resigned. "I had my hands full. Dad had trouble keeping a job, which made a roof over our heads an ongoing challenge. When I was old enough I got a job. I was determined to go to college. It was the only way to have a better life."

Good God, he felt like a selfish, shallow jerk. He'd thought he'd had it rough, had given his parents a pile of grief growing up because of it. This woman had become a caretaker to her father when she should have been playing with dolls.

"And did you? Go to college, I mean?" Starting out in college had definitely not been *his* finest hour, but the life lesson was one he'd never forget.

"Yeah. I was doing pretty well, until—" She looked down, and a muscle in her delicate jaw jerked.

"What?"

"I got pregnant with Janie and had to drop out." She met his gaze with the same fiercely defensive look he'd seen when she'd watched over her child. "My only regret is not graduating, but I could never be sorry about having Janie. She's the best thing that's ever happened to me."

Reading between the lines he figured she regretted other things. But what she'd revealed explained something of why she was reluctant to accept help. When you couldn't count on the two people you'd trusted most in the world, leaning on strangers wouldn't come easily.

He reached across the table and took her hand in his own. "You are a remarkable woman, Courtney Albright."

"Not really."

He didn't argue with her because he didn't like what he was feeling. Respect for her was a no-brainer. Against the odds, this woman had made a life for herself, welcomed a child into it, lost her husband and now carried the burden of raising her daughter all alone. Of course he respected her.

What troubled him was the possibility that he felt something more than admiration. Attraction was an A-word too, and it was growing stronger every time he saw her. If he was as smart as everyone told him, he'd get on that plane she'd been trying to get him on. He'd get out of Walnut River before this turned into something that got him into the same kind of trouble he'd found in college.

He'd fallen for a girl and she'd needed his help. When the dust settled, he'd been the one in hot water, and she'd walked away unscathed. Then she'd dumped him. That trouble had cost him more than time, money and his innocence.

That trouble had messed up his life.

Chapter Four

David had been driving his rented BMW around town for hours and not just because the car was sweet. He couldn't remember the last time he'd had so much time on his hands. After the disaster in his first year of college, his father had cut him off financially and every hour of every day every year afterwards had been consumed with classes, study and working to survive. Something he had in common with Courtney. At least his father hadn't been an alcoholic. Work had been James Wilder's obsession of choice.

After school, David had been consumed with keeping himself too busy to think, repaying student loans and building his practice. If he had less testosterone and more common sense, he would be on a plane back to that fabulous life in California.

Why, suddenly, was he resisting it? Why was he still here?

He passed Buns 'n' Burgers and a vision of Courtney's smiling face flashed into his mind. She was a beautiful woman and he had wanted very much to kiss her. After taking her back to the hospital, he'd spent a lot of time thinking about it. Maybe if he kissed the living daylights out of her, he could move on. If he didn't, his weakness for damsels in distress might rear its ugly head and land him in trouble again. It was something else he was thinking too much about since coming home.

That thought made David execute a quick right turn and whip the Beamer into the hospital parking lot located in front of the older structure. The new tower was visible behind it. He got out of the car, locked the doors and walked into the lobby.

His brother, Peter, had his office in the same hospital where their father had once worked. Growing up in this town, David had pushed the envelope and tried to shake things up. For some reason he was glad that very little had changed. Including this building. Maturity was a funny thing.

Not much was different—lobby, gift shop, information desk and signs pointing the way to the different ancillary departments. It smelled of floor polish, antiseptic and the fragility of life. Nostalgia enveloped him as he entered the elevator and proceeded to his brother's office on the fourth floor.

As he walked down the hall, David was bombarded by memories of this place. Very often, to see his father at all, he'd come here. He'd been a "fit in" between patients, rounds, emergencies and paperwork. He was all grown up now and it shouldn't still bother him. But ignoring the knot in the center of his gut and its connection to the past wasn't going to happen. Maybe he wasn't so mature after all.

David walked into the office and looked around the waiting room. Unlike his own professionally decorated offices in Beverly Hills, this one had generic chairs and tables, inexpensive prints on the walls and a TV mounted in the corner. Peter Wilder was older by four years, but that wasn't the only reason they hadn't been close growing up. Each of them reacted to their environment in their own way. His brother had followed in their father's footsteps. David had chosen a wilder path, no pun intended. He wondered if Peter's way was working for him or if he felt a similar emptiness.

When he stepped into Peter's private office, his brother looked up and grinned. "The prodigal son returns."

Shades of his own thoughts. "Hi."

David remembered people saying that the two Wilder boys looked a lot alike, but that's where the resemblance ended. Peter had set a high bar and David had suffered in comparison. More than once his father had asked why he couldn't be more like his older brother. Peter's hair was cut short and combed conservatively. His own was short but styled by running his fingers through it. Peter wore a shirt, tie and slacks under his lab coat unless he was doing his E.R. rotation. David was a jeans kind of guy with an incredibly successful practice. But he couldn't shake the feeling that he was missing something.

"Do you have a minute?" David asked.

"Of course. Glad you stopped by. Have a seat." Peter indicated the two chairs in front of his desk.

"Thanks." David took the one on the left because nine out of ten people would have gone to the right. Old habits died hard. "How've you been?"

"Good. I didn't expect to see you again so soon after Dad's funeral."

"Yeah." The knot in David's chest tightened.

"I wish the visit was under more pleasant circumstances. Thanks for coming by to look in on Janie Albright."

"I was in New York for a conference anyway."

"It was clear when that little girl was brought into the E.R. that her case was more complicated than we could handle. Courtney is part of our hospital community. On top of that, she's a widow struggling to make ends meet."

"I gathered that." And a whole lot more.

"How's Janie?"

"I did the superficial repairs and they're healing nicely. But she'll need another surgery for the more complicated reconstruction."

Peter frowned as he nodded. "From what I understand about her circumstances, that will be tough on Courtney. Besides the medical costs, there's no one on staff here at the hospital who can handle that kind of procedure. It will add expenses that she can't afford."

"I can recommend an expert in plastics as close to Walnut River as possible."

"I'm sure Courtney would appreciate that." Peter thought for a moment. "The hospital might have some programs to assist her financially. I'll check into that." He leaned back in his chair and linked his fingers over his flat abdomen. "So, how does it feel being back here?"

"The truth?"

"I'd expect nothing less."

"Weird," David said, not sure how to put it into words. "Brings back memories of Dad."

"From the expression on your face I gather the memories aren't good ones."

David glanced up. "Some good. Some not so good. Some downright bad."

"You just described life, little brother."

David laughed. "I guess so."

"Do you want to talk about what happened between you and Dad?"

"Not really." What was the point? His father was gone, along with any chance of making things right. The emptiness inside him opened just a little wider. "But I would like to talk about the hospital."

"I'm glad you brought it up."

"Oh?"

Peter leaned forward and folded his hands on his desk. "It's nice having Ella here—on a personal and a professional basis."

David tamped down an odd feeling of third-man-out and reminded himself that he had a pretty great life. "Yeah."

Of all the siblings, only Anna and David had chosen to live elsewhere. The thought of his adopted sister didn't bring back warm memories. In fact, life as he'd known it had changed dramatically when his parents took her in. Again he had the feeling he should be over it, but couldn't quite pull that off.

"Ella's a damn fine surgeon and her specialty is a welcome addition to the staff here at General. We needed someone in orthopedics."

"You're lucky to have her. Although, from what I've seen it's good for her, too. This is a terrific facility."

"I'm very proud of it," Peter said, intensely serious. "So was Dad."

David felt a twinge of regret that his father had been pleased with this hospital—a *building*—and not his own son. For the third time his inner child was acting like a child. Nothing like a trip down memory lane to make a guy feel all grown up, he thought ruefully. It was time to get out of here.

"That's great," he said, standing. "I'm sorry I can't stay longer, but—"

"Peter, I—"

The female voice made David turn and in the doorway stood Bethany Holloway. He remembered meeting the beautiful redhead with big blue eyes at Peter's cocktail party. She was a member of the hospital's Board of Directors.

"I'm sorry, Peter. Didn't mean to bother you. I didn't know David was here. I'll come back—"

"No." Peter stood. "Don't go."

"Are you sure?" When he nodded, she moved closer. "Nice to see you again, David."

"Same here."

Peter came around the desk and slid an arm around her waist as he drew her close and kissed her cheek. "You're not bothering me. Just the opposite. You're a sight for sore eyes."

"Your eyes saw me earlier this morning," she reminded him, a sparkle in her eyes.

David wondered when that morning his brother had seen Bethany, because if he had to guess, he figured they'd been in bed when the looking happened.

"My eyes can never get enough of you," Peter said, smiling down at her.

David knew they were engaged to be married, but even if he hadn't, the love shining on their faces was there for all the world to see. He could compare his career success to Peter's and come out a winner, but he envied his brother's obvious happiness and contentment. Again he suffered by comparison.

"Did I congratulate the two of you at the party?"

"You did. But thanks again. I'm a very lucky man." Peter gazed lovingly at his fiancée for a moment, then asked, "So what's up?"

"Stuff with the hospital," she said vaguely, sending a wary look in David's direction.

"It's okay to talk in front of David. He's just passing through. Besides, I have a feeling whatever it is won't be kept quiet for long."

"What's going on?" David asked.

"The easier question is what's not," Peter said ruefully. "First of all, there's a company—Northeastern HealthCare— that's making noises about taking over the hospital."

"That's bad?" David asked.

"Only if you're concerned that the standard of patient care Dad instituted here at the hospital will suffer. Their bottom line is a dollar sign."

"It's a rhyme," Bethany said. "And not in a good way."

"No kidding." Peter sighed. "So what brought you in here to bother me?"

She gave him a sassy look before saying, "A reporter from the *Walnut River Courier* just called me. He wanted a source on the record to confirm rumors of insurance fraud connected with Walnut River General's billing practices."

"What did you say?" Peter asked.

"I told him you were personally responsible for double-dipping and billing Medicare for procedures never performed."

"Beth—"

She looked at David and burst out laughing. "Did you know your brother can't take a joke?"

"So you never had that sense of humor surgically implanted?" David asked.

"Great." Peter shook his head. "It's not bad enough I have to take it from the woman I love. Now you're piling on?"

"What are brothers for?"

"Helping fend off a hospital takeover for one thing," Peter said grimly.

Before David could respond to that, Bethany said, "There's more to worry about than just the takeover. This reporter thing worries me."

"Why?" Peter asked, frowning.

"I think someone is leaking information to the press. He was citing cases, Peter. Enough of his facts were right to put a doubt in anyone's mind. Enough were wrong to cast a shadow on the integrity of Walnut River General. Either way it's the bad stuff that makes page one. Retraction is an afterthought in the classifieds. Negative publicity could make Northeastern HealthCare's takeover easier to pull off and cost them less money when they do. None of that works in our favor."

"I see your point," Peter said. "What did you tell the reporter?"

"Before I hung up on him I said 'No comment.'"

"Smart girl. Any inadvertent slip just gives them ammunition. It's already going to be an uphill battle to save this hospital. A David-versus-Goliath fight. No pun intended, little brother."

"Good one, Peter."

Bethany sighed as she glanced between the two of them. "Look, I'm sorry to interrupt. You don't see each other very often and I feel badly about raining on the reunion. I'm just going to leave now."

"Don't go on my account," David said. "I was just saying good-bye."

"You can't stay a little longer?" Peter said. "The last time you came home doesn't count. We buried Dad and you had to rush off."

"I know. I wish—"

"I'd like a chance to visit with you, David." Peter's gaze locked with his own. "I really mean that."

David wasn't so much surprised by his brother's sincerity as he was by his own response. Emotion welled up, intensifying the sense of isolation. "I believe you. But—"

"Just think about it, David."

"I will," he said, shaking his brother's hand. "Nice to meet you again, Bethany."

"Same here."

David walked into the hall and wished that Walnut River in general and this place in particular didn't mess with his mind so much. He was a successful plastic surgeon, not the insecure kid who'd disappointed his father. That was ancient history, a blast from the past, and had no bearing on his current life. Peter was a doctor and would understand the demanding workload. But this sudden need to connect was disconcerting and he had no doubt that the honesty Courtney had blamed on her accident was part of the catalyst.

He preferred to believe that her words, not the woman herself, were responsible for all this soul searching.

* * *

For the last couple of days Courtney had been hitching rides to and from the hospital with her friends who worked there. No one made her feel guilty, in fact just the opposite. They'd been eager to help. The guilt was a by-product of her own emotional baggage. But even that paled in comparison to her need to be with her child. She simply couldn't rest unless she could see with her own eyes that Janie was okay. She'd only spent one night in the pediatric ICU, which was a blessing.

Right now her daughter was dozing, so Courtney went downstairs to the hospital's main floor and checked in on the gift shop. No matter what was going on in her life, this was her responsibility. At least she didn't have to impose on someone for a ride to work from Janie's bedside. She made sure operating hours were staffed and checked over inventory. Everyone was pitching in, covering for her, going the extra mile to help her out. It's what she'd come to love most about this town, the hospital and her job.

On her way back upstairs, as she exited the elevator on the third floor and rounded the corner, she practically skidded to a stop. At the nurse's station David Wilder was chatting up Diane Brennan, a tall, beautiful, brunette R.N. He had his back to Courtney and she wished for powers of invisibility to walk by them and not be seen. Partly because she wasn't wearing makeup and her hair made her look like a reject from a makeover show, but also because her worn jeans and sweatshirt made her feel thrift-store poor beside his designer denim and pricey cotton shirt. Mostly, however, because it wasn't good the way her insides pulsed with excitement at the sight of him.

Diane slid him a sultry smile. "I heard the actress from that TV sitcom had her nose done. Do you know anything about it?"

"I'll never tell and there's nothing you can do to make me," he said, his flirtatious tone implying there was much she could do.

Courtney wanted to gag.

"Don't be like that. Inquiring minds want to know. Who have you done work on in Hollywood? Who has boobs by the famous Dr. David Wilder?"

His back to her, David leaned against the counter and folded his arms over his chest. "Nurse Brennan, you know that would be a violation of patient privacy. Besides, a gentleman never tells."

"And you're a gentleman?" Diane smiled up at him.

"Most of the time."

Courtney was glad, or would be really soon, that the two were so caught up in each other that neither noticed her walk by. She was crabby. Her wrist ached and she was so tired. But it was the hit to her heart that took her by surprise. Maybe that was a direct result of sharing burgers and backgrounds. She'd seen a different side to him; his vulnerability had seemed sincere. And that chink had made her feel comfortable enough to reveal some of her own painful past.

How naive could she be? He was standing there taking his sex appeal out for a spin and that was a punch-to-the-gut, catch-her-breath, hit-her-between-the-eyes moment.

A moment that opened her eyes once and for all. And just in time to avoid a full-blown crush on Dr. Delicious, she realized. And, while it had been an extraordinarily kind gesture, a clandestine milkshake for her little girl didn't change who he was. Once a playboy, always a playboy.

Courtney needed to focus her attention on her daughter, who was awake now.

"Hi, Mommy."

"Hi, baby. How do you feel after your nap?"

"Not so sleepy."

Courtney smiled. "Then, as naps go, it was a rousing success."

"I guess." Janie frowned.

"What is it, sweetheart?"

"Dr. David hasn't been to see me today."

"He probably got sidetracked." By a pair of long legs and an impressive bosom, Courtney thought. "You know he doesn't live here in Walnut River."

"He said he used to."

"That's true. But now he lives all the way on the other side of the country. In Los Angeles. Where they make TV shows and movies."

"So he fixes people there?"

"He fixes them all right," Courtney agreed. "On the west coast there's a lot of job security in designer medicine."

"What's that?" Janie asked.

"Nothing, sweetie." She sat beside the bed, rested her sling-braced arm in her lap and took her daughter's small fingers in her other hand. "You just have to be prepared for the fact that David isn't staying. He has to go back home." Janie's frown was troubling. Time to change the subject.

"What do you say, pumpkin? Are you ready to get out of here and go home to sleep in your own bed?"

"Can I?"

"Maybe soon. All the nurses say you're getting better really quick."

"I know. 'Cuz I'm the fastest."

Once Courtney had her at home, she could do some research on the Internet for a doctor to do the facial repairs. David said he'd recommend someone, but counting on that would be foolish. And somehow, she would find a way to pay for it. All she'd ever wanted for Janie was a normal life, the kind of childhood Courtney'd never had. There had been a few setbacks, learning what kind of man she'd married, then losing him overseas. But they'd survived that and they'd get past this.

"Word on the street is that there's a party in this room."

David stood in the doorway looking like temptation for the taking. "I can't believe no one invited me."

Courtney's heart bounced into her throat and her breath caught, but she managed to say, "Hi, David."

Janie giggled. "I'm not having a party."

He moved forward and stood by the bed. "I bet you're ready to have some fun."

"I think the Albright girls are going to need a little more recuperation time before we party."

"Dr. David, are you having a going-away party?" Janie asked him.

David looked at her. "Is it genetic? This thing the Albright girls have about getting rid of me?"

Her old friend Guilt nudged her. "Of course not. But you're only in town for a visit. By definition that means not permanent. So, sometime soon you're going back to your real life."

He folded his arms over his chest. "Correct me if I'm wrong, but every day, no matter where I am, is actually my real life."

"I meant back to your practice," Courtney amended, ignoring the way her pulse was jumping simply because he stood there and smelled so good.

"What's designer medicine?" Janie interrupted.

"Where did you hear that?" David didn't raise his voice, but there was a definite edge to it.

"Mommy said you have a job in security for designer medicine. What does that mean?"

Courtney had thought she'd successfully distracted Janie from her slip of the tongue, but no such luck. She wanted to crawl into a hole, curl up and come out when the coast was clear and David was clear on the other coast.

He looked at her. "Do you want to take a stab at explaining that?"

"I think not."

"There's a lot more to what I do than Botox and augmentation."

"I know that." She couldn't shake the crabby mood and knew it had something to do with witnessing him playing Dr. Don Juan at the nurses' station. One more in a growing list of reasons she would be better off when he was gone. "And I've thanked you numerous times for everything you've done for Janie."

"But I'm not all better yet, Mommy."

"I know, baby." Courtney still hadn't been able to force herself to look at her daughter's shattered cheek. Living with the guilt of what she'd done was hard enough without seeing the damage right in front of her. She brushed silky blond hair from the little girl's forehead. "But you'll be good as new before you know it."

"How?"

"What do you mean?"

A tear trickled out of Janie's good eye and her lips quivered. "Who's going to take care of me after Dr. David leaves?"

Please, please don't do this to me, Courtney thought. She could stand anything except this. How could she reassure this child when she had no idea what she was going to do? Tears burned the backs of her own eyes.

"Don't cry, sweetie. Don't worry. I promise you'll be fine. I'll find a doctor for you—"

"No, you won't," David interrupted

Courtney stared at him. "Excuse me?"

"I'm going to be your doctor," he said to Janie.

"You can't," Courtney answered.

"Oh?"

"I mean—how? You'll be on the other side of the country. Won't it be too inconvenient for you to take charge of her case?"

"I've been thinking," he said.

"There's a dangerous prospect."

"Be nice, Courtney."

"Sorry." She rubbed her nose. "It sounded better in my head. You were saying?"

"I've been working nonstop for a long time. I can't remember the last vacation I had."

"Walnut River isn't exactly the vacation capital of the planet."

"That's why it's perfect. Nothing to do but relax."

"What about your practice?"

"I'm not the only doctor. There are three other specialists and they'll pick up the slack."

"David, this is crazy—"

He held up his index finger. "Calling me names is not an especially good example to set," he commented, angling his head slightly toward the little girl in the hospital bed. "Do you have an objection to me being Janie's doctor?"

"Of course not. You're wonderful with her."

"So you trust me?"

"Medically speaking?"

"Yes."

"Of course I trust you." Personally, not so much.

He looked at Janie. "Would you be disappointed if I wasn't your doctor?"

"Yes," she said emphatically.

"Then, it's settled. I'm not going anywhere for a month."

"Yay!"

"Thank you, David." Courtney smiled at him and squeezed Janie's fingers.

As far as good news/bad news scenarios went, this was a classic. The worry of who would fix her daughter's face was no longer an issue. But Joe Albright had taught her that deeds come with a price. She had to conclude that David had an agenda.

All she could do was hope that whatever he wanted wasn't more than she could afford to pay.

Chapter Five

Smart men learned from their mistakes, and David considered himself a pretty smart man. Until now.

The next day he was still trying to figure out what he'd been thinking to volunteer his services. Courtney Albright was his personal train-wreck-in-waiting and ever since meeting her he couldn't seem to jump the track. Apparently he'd dumbed down since returning to Walnut River. What else would explain his offering to be Janie's doctor? He didn't owe them anything just because of his father's friendship. But when Janie had cried and Courtney had struggled not to, he couldn't hold back the words.

At midmorning he left his first-floor guest room at the Walnut River Inn. With its four-poster cherrywood bed, wallpaper in mauve with steel-blue flowers and stripes and a cream-colored porcelain sink and shower, the place was a little feminine for his taste. Of the eight guest rooms, it was the most expensive and that gave him great satisfaction because his father had once said he wouldn't amount to anything. He drove away from the picturesque gardens with their sculpted boxwoods and went to the hospital to see his patient. His only patient.

That felt weird.

Fourteen-hour days and as many procedures as he could fit into those hours were the norm. Keeping busy was his life. When he took a break from the routine, he did it in a third world country where he could make a difference to poor people without access to medical intervention. He worked fast to help as many as possible. It also meant there wasn't time to get personally involved with patients or their families. But he was involved now. What else did you call putting your life on hold for a little girl with facial trauma and her pretty mother with sass to spare?

When he arrived at the hospital, he went directly to the pediatric floor. He walked into Janie's room and was surprised not to see Courtney there. That was different. He hadn't realized he'd been looking forward to seeing her until he didn't.

"Hey, beautiful." He smiled at Janie. "How are you feeling today?"

She lifted her arm with its hot-pink cast. "It hardly hurts at all. Dr. Ella said that's good."

"She's right."

Janie nodded. "And my chin itches. Where you fixed it. But I'm not scratchin'."

"Good girl." In his opinion she was ready to leave the hospital, but he wanted to talk to her mother about that first. "Where's your mom?"

"The nurse came in and told her to go to the cafeteria and eat."

He wondered if she'd put up a fight with someone besides him. "Okay. You sit tight. I'm going to talk to her."

The cafeteria was in the hospital's basement and he took the elevator down. When the doors opened, he walked the short distance. Even if the route hadn't been familiar, the smell of food would have led him in the right direction.

He'd seen his share of hospital dining areas and knew they were pretty much all the same. But when he rounded the corner and walked in, he was swamped by déjà vu. The open room had the requisite tables and chairs, steam tables and salad bar. A sign featured the day's entrees.

Not much had changed from when he was a kid having lunch with his father. It was like every other cafeteria except that along with bad food and generic decoration, this one served up memories.

He felt a whack in the center of his chest that didn't ease until he spotted a familiar blonde sitting by herself. Since it was too early for lunch, the room was nearly empty. He watched her as he moved closer and the dark circles beneath her eyes tugged at him.

"Mind if I join you?" he asked, stopping beside her.

"Of course not. Good morning. How are you?"

"Great. And you?" She looked tired. He didn't like that he'd noticed, partly because he wanted to fix it. Mostly it was because he shouldn't notice at all. He never got this close.

"I'm fine, thanks."

He pulled out the chair across from her and sat. "Janie told me the nurse ordered you to eat something." Looking at her barely touched ham sandwich, he added, "Looks like following orders isn't your thing."

"I'm not very hungry." She took a sip from her coffee cup.

He glanced around, trying to decide if the walls had always been that color of green. "When I was a kid, I used to think the food here was the best."

"So your folks kept you on a diet of bread and water?" she teased.

"No. When I was in trouble, my punishment was losing the privilege of lunch with my dad."

"Ah." She nodded knowingly. "It was the company, not the cuisine."

"Something like that."

"Were you a naughty little boy who was disciplined often?"

"I followed Peter the Perfect and my mother wasn't ready for me," he said. His mother had died of cancer five years ago, but David had never felt he'd lived up to her expectations any more than he had his father's. He couldn't remember her being anything but moody and depressed. Whether it was the truth or not, he had the sense that she blamed him for his father not being around. "Having lunch here was the best way to spend time with my father. He was at the hospital more than home."

"I got that feeling," she said almost reverently. "I used to see him here a lot. In fact, I still half-expect him to walk in and join me for a cup of coffee."

"That must mean you work a lot. Where's Janie when you're here?"

"Day care after school. Summers and holidays are more complicated, but I have a good support system to pick up the slack." She looked pensive for a moment, then said, "I wish—"

"What?"

"Nothing."

He studied her for a moment and thought he saw regret in her expressive brown eyes. If anyone should recognize the emotion, it was him. He had regrets to spare. "For what it's worth, now that I'm a doctor, I understand that my father needed to be here for his job."

Defensiveness slid into her expression. "Managing the hospital gift shop isn't in the same league with saving lives, but it's a service that patients and visitors both appreciate. We're all on the same team in terms of patient satisfaction and well-being. When someone has no visitors, I make sure to send flowers, or a stuffed animal or a balloon bouquet. Something to let them know they're not alone."

Her tone was normal, conversational, but he felt the slight edge. He remembered it from when she'd first told him she didn't work with patients, as if her job wasn't as important. He'd never meant to diminish her in any way and the yearning to touch her was overwhelming.

He reached over and took the fingers of her good hand into his own. "State of mind is an important part of the healing process. The patients are lucky to have you."

Her guarded gaze slid from his to their joined hands, but she didn't pull away. "So, you were looking for me?" His expression must have been blank because she added, "You said Janie told you where to find me."

"Right." With an effort, he dragged his gaze away from her mouth and the overwhelming desire to kiss her. "I'm discharging Janie from the hospital."

"She can go home?" Her expression was both pleased and fearful. "Is she ready?"

He nodded. "For now everything medically necessary has been done. She's on the mend and home is the best place to build up her strength. It's familiar and comfortable. Normal."

"There's no place like home?" she said wryly.

"Exactly."

"What about the other doctors who looked after her?"

"I'm the point man on her case. Ella signed off on her release so the final decision is up to me."

And why he'd offered to take over her case was as big a mystery now as it had been when the words came out of his mouth yesterday. He remembered Ella telling him the night of Peter's cocktail party that he'd do the right thing where Janie was concerned. But was it right for him? Every time he saw the little girl, she got to him just a little more. And her mother...

Courtney had accused him of having demons, but that was the pot calling the kettle black. Otherwise she wouldn't use crabbiness the way a crab uses its protective shell. On top of that, she was under a lot of stress—worried about her child's future and how to pay for the best medical care that would ensure a bright one. The more she'd pushed him away, the more he'd wanted to help.

Smart man, stupid choices.

Courtney blew out a long breath. "Wow. Okay. I—" She ran her fingers through her silky blond hair.

"What's wrong?"

"Nothing. This is great news. I just have a million things going through my mind."

"Like?"

"I don't want to bother you with it."

"If I didn't want to know, I wouldn't have asked," he said.

"I have to speak with someone in patient services about arranging transportation home." She held up the blue sling cradling her injured arm. "Even if I could drive, I don't have a car. Good thing Walnut River General provides the assistance."

She was trying to push him away again. And again he dug his heels in. "I'll drive you home."

"You've already done so much for us, I don't want to take advantage." She shook her head. "I can't ask you to chauffeur us."

"You didn't ask. I volunteered."

"Surely you have better things to do."

"Not really. I'm on vacation."

"Wouldn't you rather take a cruise?" she asked.

"I get seasick. It's not pretty."

Her gaze narrowed skeptically. "Have you ever been on a cruise?"

"Okay. No. But I earned this time off and I should get to decide how to spend it."

"Don't you want to do something more exotic than drive us home?"

She was giving him an out and a voice inside was warning him to take it. But, as David stared into Courtney's big brown eyes, he couldn't think of a single thing he'd rather do.

After the discharge paperwork was completed, they were finally on their way home. Courtney wasn't sure whether to be relieved. Winter had robbed the trees of their leaves and the branches stood out like dark sticks against the gloomy gray sky. She lived in a "mature" section of Walnut River, where average working-class people owned homes. Big maples, sycamores and elm trees lined the streets and she thought it charming and quaint.

"Turn right on Maple. It's the fourth house," Courtney directed David, very glad the ride was almost over. She wasn't sure how much longer she could smell his amazing cologne and stare at his gorgeous profile and not embarrass herself somehow. Her hormones were jumping like toddlers on sugar overload.

He pulled up to the curb in front of an older three-story house in which each floor had been converted to a separate apartment.

"I know this area," he said, turning off the ignition. "Riverdale."

She was surprised. "Really?"

"My grandmother had a house nearby and now my sister, Ella, lives in it. It's a little Cape Cod over on Cedar."

Must be nice to have family who'd give you a head start on life, Courtney thought. She didn't feel sorry for herself any more. It was unproductive and a waste of energy. So this slip could only be blamed on a stressful couple of days.

"You must have some wonderful memories of growing up here," she said.

He looked around and frowned. "Not all wonderful, but definitely memories."

That made her curious. "It's a great neighborhood. I rent the top-floor apartment."

"Because it's the best?" he asked.

"Nope. The cheapest," she answered honestly.

He got out and came around to her side of the car, then opened her door. He held out his hand to help her and she put her fingers into his. The warmth and strength burrowed inside her, lighting up a bleak and desolate place. Strength and support were two things she'd learned never to expect from a man. Either she was doomed to disappointment or there was a price to pay. It wasn't self-pity or pessimism, more an educated guess based on experience.

Standing on the sidewalk, David glanced over his shoulder and looked up to the top floor of the tall structure. He met her gaze. "That's a lot of stairs."

"It's how I keep my girlish figure," she said.

One eyebrow rose as he checked her out from the top of her head to the tips of her sneakers. "I mean this in the very best possible way—it's definitely working. People in L.A. spend a small fortune on Pilates and yoga when all they need is stairs."

The compliment and approval in his eyes did dangerous things to her insides and she figured it was time to run for cover. "I'd better get Janie upstairs." Checking the rear seat, she saw that the child had fallen asleep. "I should have known. She was too quiet back there. I guess I'll have to wake her."

"Don't," he said. "I'll carry her up."

"It's three flights of stairs," she reminded him.

He tilted his head. "Are you challenging my manhood?"

Her gaze slid to the center of his chest and the navy sweater that covered it. Over his collared shirt and jeans it was a decidedly preppy look that worked for her as well as his bad-boy-biker one. But which was the real David Wilder?

By any standard he was a incredibly masculine and exceptionally handsome man. Any challenge to his manhood was an exercise in futility.

"Heaven forbid I would insult you. It's just that this is above and beyond the call of volunteer duty."

"I'm also her doctor. And I prescribed rest."

Courtney studied him. She got the feeling that he would meet her stubborn and raise her an obstinate or two. The thing was, she really didn't want to wake Janie. "I sense this is a battle I'm going to lose."

He grinned. "Smart girl."

He quietly opened the back passenger door and undid Janie's seatbelt before gently lifting her into his arms. The sight of him holding her child made Courtney's chest hurt and tears sting the backs of her eyes. It showed her what Janie was missing out on. It didn't matter that her own father, the one man who should have loved her the most, would never have been there for her even if he'd lived. Courtney's heart broke because she couldn't give Janie that most important thing— a father's love and support.

She couldn't stand for David to see her weakness and reached into the backseat to pull out the plastic bag that the nurses had put Janie's things into. Then she took the lead, unlocking the outside door to the building. She started up the stairs and stopped on the first landing.

"Are you okay?" she asked.

"Fine."

They took the second set of stairs and she glanced back. "Still okay?"

"Yes."

When they got to the top floor, she unlocked her door and opened it. "Home sweet home," she whispered.

He walked inside and looked around. "Very nice," he answered quietly. "Where's Janie's room?"

She motioned for him to follow, then she walked through the small living room, turning on lights to chase away the gloom. "It's the first doorway on the left."

She went in ahead of him and pulled down Janie's rosebud comforter and the pink blanket and sheet. David settled her on the mattress, then gently pulled the bedclothes over her and brushed silken strands of hair off the child's cheek. Along with the curtains and accessories, almost everything in this room was a shade of pink. In this environment a lot of men would look out of place, but not David. If anything, he looked bigger, broader, more rugged—more manly. And somehow that added balance.

They walked back to the living room and he met her gaze. "I thought my room at the inn was girly, but it has to be said that your daughter is definitely in a pink zone."

"Her favorite color," she said, shrugging.

He studied the room. "And yours is green."

"And gold and brown." Earth tones. She followed his gaze. "I painted and I picked out that fabric to recover the sofa. And I made the throw pillows." She pointed to the chocolate-brown trim. "They match the accent wall."

He glanced around and didn't look shocked or appalled. Maybe surprised in a good way. "You recovered the sofa?"

"Someone threw it away and I could still see possibilities." Plus she'd needed to furnish this place on very little money. "I also found the coffee and end tables and refinished them."

"It's charming."

"Is that your way of saying you hate it without saying you hate it?"

He looked serious. "That's my way of saying this is a

beautiful and inviting room. You're a very talented decorator."

"Thank you." She chose to believe he meant that. "What's your place like? I mean in L.A."

He frowned as he glanced around again. "Condo. Lots of space. Chrome and glass."

Sounded cold to her. As if there'd been any doubt, it proved they were oil and water, fire and ice—all things that don't mix. Normally she'd have let it pass, but he'd insinuated himself into her world and she wanted to know more about him.

"So tell me why a famous Beverly Hills doctor like yourself would make a long-distance house call?"

"Believe it or not I care about people."

Courtney felt an unpleasant twinge in her chest when she remembered him flirting with the tall, pretty nurse at the hospital. "Women-type people?" she asked before she could stop the words.

"*All* types of people. As I said before, plastics isn't just about big boobs and nose jobs."

She remembered the defensive look on his face when Janie had mentioned designer medicine. Now she was curious. "So tell me what plastics *is* about."

"It's about helping people feel better about themselves. I do procedures on men as well as women because the way someone looks on the outside can effect positive changes on the inside."

"How so?"

"Looking the best you can builds self-esteem and confidence. It's especially true when someone has catastrophic facial trauma."

"Like Janie—"

"Yes." He put a finger beneath her chin and nudged it up. "I've seen worse injuries than Janie has. This is the absolute, honest truth, Courtney. I promise that I will make your daughter's face whole—"

When he stopped, Courtney got a bad feeling. "What is it?"

"Her dimples," he said.

"What about them?"

"After the surgery, she won't have a matching set."

Courtney touched her own cheek. From the time Janie was a baby, she'd always told her she had dimples just like Mommy's. It was part of their identity and it was her fault Janie's would be altered.

"You can't fix it?" she whispered.

He blew out a long breath. "No. We're trying to perfect the technique, but haven't been successful so far. But I promise, no one who didn't know her before will notice anything except that she has a dimple on one cheek."

That was good. People wouldn't stare at her child out in public. It was a change, nothing more, she told herself. She swallowed hard and nodded. "Thank you, David. For everything."

"You don't have to thank me. I told you, I care about people."

"I believe you. Until now—with Janie—I don't think I truly understood what you do. Is it too late to take back every snarky remark?"

"I'll have to think about that," he said.

"While you're thinking, keep in mind that I didn't mean to sound ungrateful." What she'd meant to do was keep a distance between them. Here, in her little place, it was a bad time to realize she was failing miserably. "I think the strain of everything is getting to me."

"Define *everything*."

"Finances, for one." She moved over to the sofa and sat down. "My budget is stretched to the breaking point under the best of circumstances and this gives a whole new meaning to *breaking point*."

"I understand."

"If you hadn't so generously offered your services, I honestly don't know what I'd have done. But that's just one of my problems. My car is in pretty bad shape, if not completely totaled. They're going to let me know. I've already missed several days of work which I can't afford."

"Peter might be able to help you out."

When he sat beside her she felt the warmth of his body even though he wasn't touching her. She shivered and it had nothing to do with the cold outside and everything to do with the man inside.

"Maybe he could do something," she said thoughtfully. "As the acting Chief of Staff."

"So why do you still look so worried?"

"There's a rumor that the hospital is going to be taken over by a corporation."

"Peter told me." He leaned forward and put his elbows on his knees as he looked at her. "Change isn't always bad."

"No?"

"They could bring in a lot of research dollars and capital for new equipment and staff. If that were the case, there might be a plastic surgeon here in Walnut River and you wouldn't need me."

She didn't want to need him and had a bad feeling that it was becoming more personal than professional. "It's not just about health care. With a corporation we'd lose the human component. Peter wouldn't be able to do anything about my situation because it's all spreadsheets, computers and the bottom line. Change is almost always bad."

"Has anyone ever told you you're a glass-is-half-empty kind of person?"

She had good reason. Life had knocked her around and it was much easier not to have expectations. "At the risk of looking even more pessimistic, have you ever seen a corporate takeover where no one lost their job?"

He was quiet for several moments before answering, "No."

"I'm taking online business courses to get my degree. That will open up employment opportunities."

"That can't be easy to do while raising a child and working full-time."

"It's a challenge. But the full-time job is the most important. If I lose mine, I'm not sure I could get another one where I could make enough to support the two of us. And it will take me another year and a half before I can get my degree. I really need my job."

"I understand your concern."

"Even with it, I'm not sure how I'm going to handle our medical bills. I'm not even sure yet how I'm going to be able to go to work until she's feeling better."

"I can help."

The last thing she needed was to be further in his debt. "I have a support system. I just need to figure out what to do."

"You just said you've been under a strain the last few days. I can make this one easy."

"That's very generous of you, but—"

"Don't say it."

"What?"

"Anything negative."

"It never crossed my mind." She sighed. "The thing is, I already owe you more than I can repay."

"I'm not asking for anything." He looked at her. "You'd be doing me a favor."

"Oh, please."

"Seriously. I find myself with time on my hands."

"Because you volunteered—"

"Because I'm on vacation."

"Mommy?" Janie stood in the doorway, rubbing her eyes.

"Hi, baby. Did we wake you up?" Courtney held out her arms and the little girl walked over and crawled into her lap. "How do you feel?"

"Sleepy. I like my bed better than the hospital one."

"I know." She kissed her daughter's forehead.

"Let's let Janie decide," David suggested.

"'Cide what?" the little girl asked.

"Your mother has to go to work, and you're not ready to go back to school yet. And I don't have anything to do. What do you think about spending some time with me?"

"I can see if Mrs. Arnold downstairs can stay with you," Courtney suggested.

Janie made a face then met his gaze. "Can we play cards?"

"Sure," he said.

"What about milkshakes?" the little conniver asked, perking up.

"You drive a hard bargain, but I think it could be arranged."

"Okay. You can stay with me." Janie slid out of her mother's arms and scooted into David's lap. When she rested her cheek on his chest as if she'd been doing it for years, his strong arms folded around her as though she belonged there.

"I guess it's settled," David said, a smug tone to his voice.

"I guess."

How she'd love to relax and just let it be settled, but that couldn't happen. Her obligation to this man was mounting steadily and that was hard enough for her to take. But why was he being so generous to her when he'd ignored his father and family for so long? What kind of man was he? Charming playboy or knight in shining armor?

Either man could break her heart if she let him.

Chapter Six

"Dr. David, my ears are tired."

"Okay." He closed the book of fairy tales, pink cover of course, and looked down at Janie.

"I'm bored."

It was just a few days ago that Courtney had reacted so emotionally to those words. A hint of normal he understood better after spending a day with this munchkin.

"Do you want to play Monopoly? Or Scrabble?"

She shook her head, then crawled into his lap and rested her left cheek on his chest. The innate trust in the act squeezed his heart. At that moment if she'd asked for the moon, he'd have moved heaven and earth out of the way to get it for her.

"I guess I'm not much fun," he said, wishing he knew better how to entertain her.

"Yes, you are fun. I'm glad you stayed with me."

"I'm glad you're glad."

She sighed. "I don't think Mommy was very glad."

That was the understatement of the century. Yesterday when he'd brought them home from the hospital, Courtney had tried to talk him out of his offer because she didn't trust him. The truth was she probably shouldn't trust him because his motives *were* selfish. He had time on his hands and didn't look forward to doing nothing, even if he could afford to do it in the most expensive room at the Walnut River Inn. So Janie was actually doing him a favor.

"Thanks for going to bat for me with your mom," he told her.

"What's that mean?" Janie asked, looking up. There was something about a little girl in pink sweats and fuzzy slippers that made him want to stand between her and all the bad stuff in the world.

The lamp on the table beside them had little crystals dangling from the fluted beige shade. He liked it. In fact, he liked everything about this place, including—especially—its occupants. He'd paid more for a desk lamp than everything in this apartment had probably cost, yet there was something intangible here that made him feel good—something that money couldn't buy.

He smiled at the little girl. "*Going to bat* means you stuck up for me, pal. I appreciate it."

"It's okay." She caught her top lip between her teeth as a pensive expression filled the face so like her mother's.

"What's wrong, kiddo?"

She met his gaze with her one good eye. "I didn't tell Mommy, but I lifted up the bandage and looked."

With an effort, he kept his own expression neutral and tried to read hers. "Okay."

"My face looks gross." Her lips trembled.

"You have a serious injury, sweetie, but I'm going to make you just like before the accident."

A tear slid down her uninjured cheek. "What if you can't?"

He rubbed her arm then linked his fingers to snuggle her closer. "Have I ever lied to you?"

She thought for a moment. "No. In the hospital you said it would be a little pinch and then it wouldn't hurt. And it didn't."

"I'll always tell you the truth." He rested his chin on top of her head. "I can fix your face, but it will be a little different from before."

"How?" she said, turning a worried look up at him.

"I can't give you back your dimple."

"What if the kids at school make fun of me?"

She needed reassurance but this was way out of his league. He worked on kids, but he got in and out without emotional involvement. Not this time. Janie had stolen a piece of his heart. This required tact and diplomacy beyond his limited scope. Searching for the right words, he remembered having stitches as a kid.

At a neighbor's, he'd fallen on a sprinkler and took a chunk out of his knee down to the fat layer. The woman had turned white and he'd thought she'd pass out. Then his dad was there, telling him that there would be a scar, but that was cool for guys. Janie was a little girl. What would his father have told her?

"The kids at school are all going to be jealous of you," David finally said.

"Really?"

He nodded. "The girls will envy you because all the boys are going to think you look very mysterious with one dimple. You can tell them the other one was stolen by an evil sorcerer until your true love's first kiss."

"And I'll live happily ever after, like the story you read me?"

"Just like that." He met her gaze. "I promise you this, pal. It will take some time to heal, but eventually no one will ever know from looking at you that you were in a car accident." When she said nothing, he wished he could hug her tight enough to make her believe.

Finally he asked, "Do you trust me?"

She nodded and with her good hand she plucked the cotton of his white shirt. "Dr. David, how come you can't stay here in Walnut River forever?"

"Because my work isn't here," he explained.

"You could work here," she suggested. "You're going to make me better. You could make other people better, too."

"It's not that easy, squirt."

"Why not?" She rested her elbow on his midsection.

It was pointy and poked a rib, but he sucked it up because she was comfortable. "I have a practice in Beverly Hills. People there are depending on me."

"Aren't there other doctors there? Can't people go to someone else?"

"There are lots of doctors, but there are people who want to come to me. I've spent a lot of years working hard to be the best."

She thought about that for a few moments. "Mommy and me would have had to go somewhere to get my face fixed if you didn't stay. If you're the best, wouldn't people come here?"

"It's possible, but—"

"Then you could stay," she said, as if the problem were solved.

"Not forever, pal."

"I guess I knew that." She sighed. "Nobody stays."

"What do you mean?"

"My daddy had to go. Mommy said he wanted to stay with us but he had to be a soldier. Then he had to go to the war. When I was four, he didn't come back."

David had promised not to lie to her, but there were times the whole truth wasn't necessary. "Your father was a brave man."

"I guess." She shrugged. "I don't 'member him."

"You have that picture by your bed. I saw it when I tucked

you in." David remembered the good-looking guy in his army uniform. "I'm sure your mom talks about him."

Janie shook her head. "She won't. It makes her sad."

"She must love him very much," he commented. There were issues, but after all this time Courtney was still alone. Because she was still in love with her husband?

David knew that shouldn't make a difference to him one way or the other. He wouldn't lie to Janie and it probably wasn't smart to lie to himself. The fact that Courtney might still have deep feelings for her husband touched a nerve.

It was time to change the subject. "So, you like me better than Mrs. Arnold?"

Janie wrinkled her nose. "She snores when her soap operas come on TV."

"Since you kept me too busy to fall asleep, that wasn't an issue." David looked outside and noticed it was almost dark. Time flies when you're having fun. He realized it *had* been a good time. He stood with Janie in his arms. "Okay. Your mom will be home soon. Since I'm the only one around here with two good arms, I'll cook dinner."

"I can help," Janie offered.

"Can you set the table?"

"Yes." Her silky blond hair fell forward when she nodded vigorously. "Can you really cook?"

"I can dial the phone."

He didn't think his heart could melt more, but her sunny smile finished it off.

It was six-thirty when Courtney got to the door of her apartment and she was tired clear to the bone. Walking up three flights had almost done her in. That's what she got for teasing David about his masculinity. She let herself inside and was instantly besieged by delicious smells. Her stomach rumbled and she hadn't even realized she was hungry.

When Janie spotted her, she said, "Mommy's home."

David was in the kitchen bending over, peering into the oven. "Hi, there," he said, glancing over his shoulder.

When he straightened, she felt a twinge of disappointment because the man had a fine backside and she'd had a spectacular view. The thought proved that she was on thin ice here. Noticing something like that hadn't happened to her in a very long time.

"Hi." She stopped beside the sofa and pressed a kiss to her daughter's forehead. "How do you feel?"

"Okay. Me and Dr. David played games and watched *Nemo* and he read my fairy-tale book. And he taught me a card game and we bet with my pretend money."

She stood up straight and met his gaze. "Tell me it's not poker."

"Am I allowed to lie this time?"

She groaned. "If I try really hard, I can find a way to believe that poker is educational."

"Of course it is. Colors, shapes and patterns."

"Right." She sniffed. "I smell something good."

"There's an Italian restaurant on Lexington that delivers. Janie already had her pizza. I hope you like ravioli in tomato cream sauce, salad with oil and balsamic vinegar and garlic bread."

"It's my favorite. How did—"

"Janie told me." He joined her beside the couch and handed her a glass of wine. "How was your day?"

He didn't say "dear." Not even close, but for some reason her mind added it. "I was busy."

Work was a snap compared to coming home to David. It was too nice. And it would be too easy to get used to having him around, too easy to look forward to seeing his incredibly handsome face at the end of a day. Too easy to start relying on him. If not for his help, she wasn't sure how she'd have gotten through this. How could she ever pay him back? You could never go wrong being gracious.

She took a sip of wine. "I hope Janie wasn't too much for you."

"Yeah, she was pretty tough to take." He lifted his chin in her direction. "I think I wore her out. But it seems she wouldn't give in to rest until you got home."

The little girl was curled into the corner of the sofa, eyes closed, breathing evenly.

"This is early even for her," Courtney said. "I'll put her to bed."

"Let me." He rounded the sofa and lifted Janie, then carried her down the hall.

That was the second time and Courtney felt she was falling into habit territory. The man lived a life of luxury on the west coast, yet he chose to stay here and help her out. She would try to believe he was doing it because he really did need a vacation.

He returned and said, "She's in for the night. Mission accomplished."

When Courtney looked at the kitchen table, she noticed it was set for one. "You're not staying?"

"I didn't want to presume."

"Oh, please. Of course you're welcome. Stay." The last word came out as a plea to her ears but she hoped he hadn't heard it that way. Later she would worry about how much she didn't want him to go.

She put another setting on the table and they sat at right angles to each other after he served up portions on the plates. For several minutes they ate in silence.

David chewed thoughtfully. "Janie said she doesn't remember her father."

"She didn't see him much. Joe moved us to Walnut River to be closer to his parents."

"Morris and Elizabeth Albright, right?"

She nodded. "You know them?"

"They were friends of my folks. Nice people."

Not to her, but that was another story. And not pretty. "We were barely settled when he enlisted in the army and went to boot camp. I was six months pregnant."

He looked surprised. "He left before Janie was born?"

"Yes. After training, he didn't want to uproot us. We stayed here and he came home when he could."

"I see."

His tone said he didn't see at all. That made two of them. Joe had insisted on getting married when she found out she was pregnant and she'd thought he was incredibly honorable and decent. He'd brought her home to his family and she'd believed for a short time that all her dreams were coming true. But when things didn't go the way he wanted, Joe left her and Janie alone.

"He was killed shortly after his second tour of duty started in Iraq."

"I'm sorry."

"Me, too." She put her fork down and took a sip of wine.

"You've made it clear that life with Joe wasn't moonlight and roses, but it still must have been hard for you. Janie told me that talking about him makes you sad."

Instantly her gaze lifted to his. "I didn't know she'd noticed."

"She's a sharp cookie," he said.

"It *was* hard. For so many reasons. Making ends meet was always difficult."

"I thought servicemen have an insurance policy."

"They do. And each soldier receives counseling before deploying to a war zone." For some reason she found herself telling him more than she intended. "Joe neglected to name me as a beneficiary on his Serviceman's Group Life Insurance. The death benefit was paid to his estate but all the money went to legal fees to straighten out the mess he left behind. There's a small amount of money monthly, but it doesn't stretch far."

David's mouth thinned. "At the risk of speaking ill of the dead, that seems a bit irresponsible."

"That was Joe." Courtney shrugged. "I was blindsided when he joined the army. She was his child. I thought he'd want a relationship with her even though he and I had…"

"What?"

She shook her head. "Doesn't matter any more."

"So between your father and your husband, you had to be independent." He took her hand. "That explains a lot about why you have such a hard time accepting help."

He didn't know the half of it. And what she'd revealed wasn't the worst, but there was no reason to say more. Her husband hadn't provided the security she'd expected, but he had taught her that she really could only count on herself. It was a lesson she'd never forget. Although she hated the reminder because it felt really good when David gently squeezed her fingers.

"Court, do you ever think maybe you're *too* strong?"

"I don't think that's possible."

"Don't you ever get tired of doing it by yourself? Don't you ever want to let someone else in?"

She shook her head. "No."

For several moments, he looked at her as he brushed his thumb back and forth over her knuckles. "I see something else in your eyes."

"I'm not sure what that is, but I can tell you for a fact that I'm glad I'm strong enough to take care of Janie and me without help."

"It must get lonely."

"I have friends. This town is my family."

He stood and drew her to her feet, too. "But is that enough?"

"Yes, I—"

"Really?"

But the intensity in his eyes stole her breath and she couldn't answer. Then he cupped her face in his hands and kissed her. The way she leaned into him was answer enough. Her arm in the sling was between them, but he still managed to fold her against the solid length of his body. He threaded his fingers in her hair and gently urged her lips more firmly to his while her heart pounded and her breathing grew ragged.

She should have put a stop to it, but couldn't seem to find the will. Disappointment coursed through her when he pulled away, then pressed his forehead to hers and sucked in air.

"I've been wanting to do that from the first time I saw you."

"Y-you have?"

He nodded. "And you can tell yourself that you're content to be alone. But when you do, remember this—I'm not the only one who's breathing hard. And that makes me pretty damn happy."

He was right. It was so good. It had been so long since she'd felt like this and she didn't want it to end. But in the next instant, he kissed her forehead and stepped back.

"What—?"

"I'd better go."

"You're leaving?" Even she heard the whispered yearning in her voice.

"You need rest and recuperation as much as Janie. Although it's a waste of breath trying to convince you." There was regret in his eyes. "If I'm here you won't relax. So I'm going." He walked to the door and opened it, then looked at her. "But make no mistake. I'll be back."

She'd heard that before, but she'd never wanted to believe it as much as she did at this moment. Which was why he was so dangerous. That and the fact that if he'd wanted to take her to bed, she'd have willingly gone. She was pretty sure he knew it, too. She could understand if that's what he wanted from her. But he'd revved up her motor then left her idling. What was up with that?

No man was this noble and she simply couldn't afford to believe that David was.

Courtney put down the phone in her office, hardly more than a closet behind the hospital gift shop with barely enough space for her desk and shelves filled with inventory. The call had been from the insurance company. It had been a week since the accident and the adjuster informed her that the car was a total loss, so transportation was one more thing to worry about. Self-pity was a waste of energy, but just this once the thought sneaked in that she just couldn't seem to catch a break.

Karen Marshall picked that moment to peek in. "Sorry to bother you, Court." She looked closer. "Something wrong?"

"The insurance company just called. My car's a goner."

"Ouch. That sucks." Karen was a twenty-year-old redhead, a college student working part-time to help with expenses.

"I'll figure something out. Did you need me? Everything okay in the shop?" Courtney asked.

"Fine. Janie's here. With Dr. Wilder's brother."

"David." True to his word, he had come back to stay with her daughter that morning.

"Yeah." Karen's blue eyes narrowed in mock censure. "You never said a word about him being a hottie."

"Sorry." She shrugged. "What's wrong?"

"Nothing as far as I know. Dr. Hot Stuff just asked me to let you know they were here."

"Thanks." Courtney glanced at the clock on her wall. "It's time for you to go to lunch. I'll cover for you."

"Thanks, Boss."

Courtney followed her employee into the shop, as always glancing at the racks of greeting cards and stuffed animals. There was a small cold case for fresh flowers and shelves of porcelain and crystal figurines. A display of miscellaneous toiletries, candy bars and snacks lined up on the shelves in front of the cash register. Everything looked tidy and stocked.

Janie ran up to her. "Hi, Mommy."

"Hi, baby," she said, snuggling the little girl against her good side. "What are you doing here?"

"She wanted to come and see you," David explained.

"Is that all?" Courtney asked the little girl.

"Mostly." After a moment she said, "While I'm here, I thought maybe I could have some cafeteria ice cream."

"She loves the soft-serve here. Go figure," she said to David. Then she looked at Janie. "I can't take you, sweetie. I have to stay here while Karen goes to lunch."

"I'll take her," Karen offered. "I haven't seen her for a long time. We can catch up."

"Can I, Mommy?"

"Sure."

"Thanks, Mommy."

"Sorry about your car, Court," Karen said, then the two of them walked out into the hospital lobby.

They moved out of sight toward the elevator to the basement. And just like that she was alone with David. The last time she'd been alone with him he'd kissed her. When she met his gaze, something in his told her he was remembering, too.

Her cheeks burned, but she ignored the feeling. That was a whole lot easier than ignoring how good he looked in his worn jeans, white shirt and battered leather jacket. His hair was mussed in that sexy, trendy way. But in his case she had a feeling it wasn't deliberate as much as how he stepped out of the shower. Thoughts of David, showers, bare skin and muscles brought more heat to her face.

"So," she said, blowing out a long breath. "It was nice of you to bring her down here."

"There's another reason. It's been a week. Her stitches are ready to come out. I talked to Peter and he says there's a suite of offices in the new tower used for visiting doctors. When Karen comes back, can you slip away for a few minutes? I figured you'd want to be there."

"Of course. She'll be nervous."

"It's the easy part. I've already talked to her about what I'm going to do and promised that it won't hurt. She'll just feel a little pull. After that there are ointments I can recommend that will expedite healing and minimize scarring."

"Okay. Thank you, David. You're wonderful with her," Courtney said. "She trusts you."

"At least one of the Albright women does."

It was too much to hope he hadn't noticed. "Yeah. Well—"

"So what's the deal with your car?" At her blank look, he said, "Karen mentioned it before she left with Janie."

"Oh. Right." She let out a long breath. "The insurance company called and my little compact flat-lined. No possibility of resuscitation."

"They'll reimburse you for the loss, right?"

"Yeah. But it wasn't worth much. The thing is, it was paid for. I have to buy a new one and a payment is not in my budget."

He rested a lean hip against the glass case where knick-knacks were displayed. "Courtney, I could loan—"

"No." She held up a hand. "You've already done enough. I'll think of something. Part-time job, maybe—"

"You're already working full-time and taking classes. And raising a child. There are only so many hours in a day."

"You think I don't know that?" Her life was a house of

cards and it was collapsing around her. "It's my problem, David. And I'll deal with it."

"How?" He ran his fingers through his hair. "What about your in-laws? The Albrights?"

"No."

"Asking them for help is not weakness. My father knew them. They're good people."

"Your father liked everyone."

"I'm sure they'd help—"

"No, they won't."

"You said the people in this town are like family. But Janie is their actual granddaughter."

"That didn't seem to make a difference to them when Joe and I got married and moved here."

He frowned. "What are you saying?"

Courtney would never forget the coldness in their eyes when they said that Joe's unfortunate choices were his to deal with and they wanted nothing to do with his mistakes.

She started to shake and was angry that even after six years the humiliation of that moment hadn't gone away. She'd told herself over and over that success was the best revenge, but it was elusive. She kept working toward it, but every time she got close something happened and she slid right back to square one and started over.

And she would do it again now. For her daughter.

She met David's puzzled gaze. "I'm saying that the Albrights made it quite clear that they didn't approve of me. I won't ask for their help or give them the satisfaction of turning me down again."

"There must be some misunderstanding."

"Not likely," she defended, rubbing her arm. Her wrist ached but it was nothing compared to the pain in her heart.

"That just doesn't sound like the people I know."

"Maybe you don't know them as well as you think."

"Maybe not." He looked angry.

She didn't know how to deal with that. Fighting her own battles had been a way of life for so long, she didn't know anything different. And she was tired. More than that, she was afraid. Afraid this was the financial hit that would sink her. Afraid to drop her guard and lean on anyone. When David's support was gone, as she knew it would be, she was terrified that she'd fall and never be able to get back up.

Kissing him was dangerous. It opened a window to her heart, showed her how much he could hurt her. All that in spite of the fact that he had a questionable sense of loyalty. He was leaving. She was counting on it, because she didn't want to care about him.

That would be the death blow to her soul.

Chapter Seven

Late the next afternoon when Courtney arrived home from work to be with her daughter, David declined another dinner invitation from Janie. It bothered him to disappoint her and disturbed him even more how much he wanted to stay and talk to her mother. Maybe kiss her again. But he had something important to do.

He drove the BMW into the long driveway lined with sycamore trees and pulled up in front of the large brick house. Morris and Elizabeth Albright had lived here for as long as he could remember, but he didn't recall ever meeting their son. Joe was about nine years younger than he was; their paths had never crossed in school, then David had left for college.

He walked up several steps to the etched-glass front door and rang the bell. Lights inside went on just before the door was answered by Elizabeth Albright, who looked to be in her late fifties.

"Hello, David," she said.

He'd called ahead. "Mrs. Albright—"

"You're grown up now. Call me Elizabeth." She stood back and pulled the door open wider. "Come in, please."

"Thank you." He looked around.

The shined-to-perfection marble floor reflected the light from an overhead chandelier. On either side of the entryway twin staircases with intricate wrought-iron spindles topped by an oak handrail curved upward to the second floor. A mahogany table held a huge vase filled with fresh star lilies, daffodils, roses and baby's breath.

She closed the door then studied him. "You look a great deal like your father."

"So I've been told."

Elizabeth Albright was a tall, elegant woman with blue eyes and blond hair—probably not naturally blond. Her skin was still good, with minimal wrinkling and age damage even though, as far as he could tell without an examination, she'd not had work done. In her black silk lounging outfit and matching low-heeled shoes, she oozed an aura of wealth and privilege that could have intimidated Courtney when she was young and pregnant. He'd believed the Albrights were a kind and generous couple who would embrace a woman like Courtney and their only grandchild. But that's not what had happened—and he was here to find out why.

"Morris is in the library. We were just about to open a bottle of wine. Will you join us?"

"Thank you."

As he followed her into a room off the entryway, the floral scent surrounded him. In winter, fresh flowers were costly and again he wondered at the apparently callous attitude toward their son's widow and his child.

"Morris, David Wilder is here."

An older man looked up from a newspaper—the *Walnut River Courier*. He looked to be in his early sixties, silver-haired and fit. He stood when David walked into the bookshelf-lined room. A fire snapped and crackled in the fireplace on one wall. Two leather loveseats faced each other perpendicular to it with a cherrywood table between them.

David walked over to the man and held out his hand. "It's nice to see you, sir."

"And you." The man had an iron grip. He indicated the seat across from himself. "Have a seat, my boy."

"Thank you." David sat and Elizabeth handed them each a glass of red wine.

Morris took a sip and nodded. "An excellent pinot. Your father would have approved."

"I wouldn't know about that." The years when he could have shared an adult relationship with James Wilder were spent not speaking at all. The waste of it twisted and echoed inside him.

"You're a doctor, too?" he asked.

"Yes, sir. I specialize in reconstructive and plastic surgery. Designer medicine." Janie had heard it from her mother, who'd probably heard it from his father. "My father *didn't* approve of my specialty."

Morris merely nodded, then said, "I was sorry to hear about your father's death. He was a good friend and I miss him."

"Thank you, sir."

Elizabeth sat beside her husband. "Your father always spoke highly of you."

David didn't know how to respond. She was simply being polite because the words couldn't possibly be true. He'd been a lousy son and a severe disappointment to his father. Now, the man who had influenced him more than any other, who he'd respected more than any other and wanted so very much to please, was gone. Death was forever. David knew there was no way to reverse the damage he'd done.

"My father tried to see only the best in people," he finally said. James Wilder had tried his damnedest and failed to make his rebel son a better person. A better person would have swallowed his pride and contacted his father before it was too late. "How did you meet my father?"

Elizabeth's sigh was so deep it seemed to come from the depths of her soul. "It was when our daughter became ill."

"I didn't know you had a daughter."

"She died of leukemia many years ago," Morris explained.

"I'm sorry." He hadn't known, but then he'd been just a kid.

"Your father was her doctor and she spent a lot of time in Walnut River General. The people there took such good care of her, made the worst time in our lives tolerable. When she died we were inconsolable. Didn't know what to do with our grief. James suggested we endow the hospital pediatric department as a memorial. We did and have been involved ever since in fundraising and charitable endeavors."

David realized his father had a way of planting the seed of compassion and generosity. It was why his own medical intervention trips to impoverished countries had seemed natural when he'd finally had the skill and training to do some good.

Elizabeth half turned toward him. "Over the years we've donated money for equipment, toys, redecoration for a child-friendly environment and scholarships. The money is administered through a trust in our daughter's name. There's a plaque at the hospital, just outside pediatrics, a dedication to the Jane Elizabeth Albright Memorial Trust."

The name got his attention. "Your daughter's name was Jane?"

"That's right," Morris said. "We had a son, too. Joe. He was killed in Iraq."

"I'm sorry for your loss," he said automatically. But David was surprised when the older man's eyes turned hard. "Actually that's the reason I've come."

"Because of Joe?" Elizabeth asked.

"In a way, yes."

"Did he do something?" Morris leaned forward, wariness in his expression. "That boy—"

"Morris, don't start. We have to take some responsibility for Joe," Elizabeth said, patting her husband's knee. "After Jane died, we indulged him, protected him too much. *Enabled him,* I think, is the politically correct term today."

"That seems a natural reaction," David commented.

"Maybe. But he became manipulative and self-centered. Because he joined the army, everyone in Walnut River thinks he's something special."

Not everyone, David thought, remembering what Courtney had said. "He gave his life for his country. I'd say that makes him pretty special."

"You're James's son, all right. Seeing only the best," Morris said. "But it was hard to see any good in Joe." He met David's gaze, man to man. "What I'm telling you stays in this room. Joining the army had something in it for Joe. I'll guarantee you that."

"How can you be so sure?"

The older man's blue eyes turned hard, angry. "He never gave up trying to get money out of us and when we went soft and gave it to him, it ran through his fingers like water. He tried everything he could to rip us off and we did everything we could think of to help him be a better man. The only thing he has left is a reputation as a hero."

"He has a daughter," David pointed out. "Janie."

Elizabeth's mouth thinned. "I still can't believe that woman had the nerve to name her child after our little girl."

"She's not 'that woman,'" David said, keeping his voice even with an effort. "Her name is Courtney Albright. She's your son's widow and Janie is your grandchild."

Morris rested his clenched fist on his knee. "Maybe I

wasn't clear enough. Our son would have done anything to extort money from us. Including bringing home a woman who claimed to be pregnant with his child. It took us a long time, but we learned not to trust him or anyone who would marry him."

"I've gotten to know Courtney pretty well," David said. "She's not the type to use people."

Elizabeth's gaze narrowed. "Don't make the mistake of falling for her, David."

Not a chance, he thought. But if Courtney was an opportunist, she was putting on a darn good act. And even if it was an act, he was painfully aware of his own weakness for a woman who needed his help. Maybe it was some whacked-out need of his to fix his own life by fixing hers. Either way, he was on guard.

"Thanks for the warning, but I can take care of myself."

"I hope so. Losing Jane broke our hearts," Elizabeth said. "Joe's machinations and schemes broke our spirit. Trusting him and anyone who was with him wasn't an option." She sighed. "At least he died with a hero's reputation. And that's the end of it. We have no wish to dredge up all the pain again."

"The last thing I want is to open old wounds. But Courtney is struggling because your son didn't follow through on his responsibilities to her or his child. He joined the army, then his carelessness left her nothing but red tape and legal fees. In spite of that, she's made a warm and loving home. She's raising a bright and happy little girl while working full-time and taking classes online to complete her degree. She's doing it by herself, but she needs help."

"She's not our problem." Morris's lips pressed together until his mouth was a tight line.

"She's the mother of your grandchild. That kind of makes it your problem."

"We have no proof that child is Joe's," Elizabeth said, her voice shaking.

"What about a DNA test?"

"I have no wish to be made a fool of again. Or disappointed again," Elizabeth said softly.

David stood. "You wouldn't be let down."

"And how can you be so sure of that?" Morris asked.

"I reconstruct faces for a living, and without bragging too much, I'm pretty good at what I do. People from across the country come to me to have work done. It's my job to study faces, bone structure, to know every curve and angle."

"Your point is?" Elizabeth stood and met his gaze.

"Janie Albright has your chin, Elizabeth, and I've seen her lift it as stubbornly as you're doing right now." He looked down at Morris. "She has your blue eyes, sir. I would stake my considerable reputation on the fact that she *is* your grand-daughter. And you're missing out on a lot if you turn your backs. Take it from someone who knows all about regrets."

Without another word, David walked to the front door and let himself out. He'd made his point and the Albrights had a lot to think about. Courtney had hinted at issues with her husband and his own parents had painted a pretty unflattering portrait of their son. That made him wonder what Courtney had gone through—and he intended to find out.

Courtney waited in the exam room for Dr. Ella Wilder. This was the moment of truth—surgery or no surgery. Obviously she was hoping for the latter. It would be the single bright spot in an otherwise sucky week. Actually, David was a bright spot, although she didn't like admitting that even to herself. After this appointment it was time to go home and the thought made her shiver. That happened every time she thought about seeing the handsome doctor, which was pretty much every day, since he was looking after Janie.

The door opened and Ella was there in her lab coat. Courtney often saw her in the gift shop, buying mints, a candy bar or bottled water. She was in her late twenties, pretty, medium height, with straight dark-brown hair worn in a bob, and warm brown eyes. In fact, her eyes seemed to sparkle more than usual.

"Courtney, hi. How are you?"

"Good, thanks."

"Let's take a look at that wrist." She removed the sling Courtney had begun to think of as an accessory to every outfit. Then she took off the temporary cast that now had room to spare and carefully examined the arm. "The swelling has gone down a lot more than I expected. We'll get another X-ray, but I'm pretty sure this is not going to need surgery. I'll put a cast on, probably for about four weeks, then we'll reevaluate."

"Thank God." Courtney let out her breath.

"I'm glad I could make you happy."

"Speaking of happy…" Courtney grinned at her.

The hospital rumor mill had been churning with tidbits about Ella and the good-looking businessman who had ended up in the hospital after losing his balance on the slippery sidewalk outside. Ella had been his doctor.

"What?" Ella looked clueless.

"You're looking especially glowing."

"Am I?" she said mysteriously.

"Duh," Courtney shot back. "The buzz is that there's a man involved. What's his name?"

"The rumor's name is J. D. Sumner." Her dark eyes radiated happiness even as a becoming blush pinkened her cheeks. "If I'm glowing, it's because love is good for the complexion."

"If love is what it takes, there's no hope for my skin."

"Don't be so pessimistic. You look great. The bruises are fading and the arm is healing nicely. How's Janie?"

"Doing great. Thanks to David. He's certainly gone above

and beyond the call of duty." And she didn't just mean his medical expertise. That kiss was way above and beyond. Courtney shook her head even as she felt the warmth in her own cheeks.

"I hear David is sticking around."

"For Janie's surgery, to repair her cheek."

Ella sighed. "I was hoping he'd change his mind about that."

"Doing the procedure?" Courtney asked, surprised.

"No. God, no. He's the best and that's what we want for Janie." She shook her head. "I was hoping he'd move back to Walnut River."

"His life isn't here any more." Courtney reminded herself of that every time that special shiver danced over her skin when she thought about him.

"For a man whose life is somewhere else, my brother is certainly—how did you put it? Going above and beyond the call of duty." Ella's eyebrow lifted knowingly.

"Me?" She tapped her chest. "I have no idea what you mean."

"I think my brother is smitten. Just today I was up in peds looking in on a patient and ran into one of the hospital's most generous patrons. She said David came to see her and it was all about you."

"Who was she?"

"Elizabeth Albright." Ella tapped her chin. "She's your mother-in-law, right?"

"Right," Courtney answered.

She was surprised her mouth worked at all after the cold that crept through her. Then anger set in and she welcomed the warmth of it to push out everything else.

Courtney walked up the three flights of stairs to her apartment and opened the door. David was sitting on the couch reading what looked like a medical publication. When she walked in, he smiled. God help her, she felt it deep down inside, where she carried the memory of his shattering kiss. It was a place she'd protected all her life. Joe had breached her defenses and that had been a disaster. But even he hadn't touched her as deeply as David, in spite of the fact that she'd seen with her own eyes that he was a flirt. She didn't want to care that he had smiled at another woman the way he was smiling at her now. But she did. It was time to put a stop to this.

She looked around the living room. "Where's Janie?"

"Taking a nap. You're home early."

"I had an appointment with Ella."

"I know, but I figured you'd go back to work. What did my sister say about your arm?"

She held up her neon-green cast. "It's healing nicely and surgery won't be necessary."

"Excellent news." He stood up, took three steps forward and pulled her into his arms for a hug.

She wanted to stay there so badly, which was why she forced herself to step away. Courtney went to the hallway and pulled the door shut. She didn't want her little girl to hear this.

"What's wrong, Court?"

She turned on him as outrage and memories of past humiliation made her shake. "How *dare* you go to see the Albrights!"

"Ah." He nodded grimly. "News still travels at the speed of light in this town."

"Ella saw Elizabeth Albright at the hospital. More likely the old bat was trolling for information. She wanted to know why in the world you'd champion someone like me."

His gaze narrowed. "What does that mean?"

"It means the Albrights didn't think much of me six years ago and there's no reason to change their minds now. Why didn't you stay out of it? You had no right to talk to them about me."

"Calm down, Court—"

"Don't patronize me, David."

Damn, she thought, as tears burned her eyes. All the painful memories rushed through her mind like a kaleidoscope of humiliation. Joe's parents had all but said she was trash—untrustworthy trash not good enough for their son. She'd been pregnant, newly married because of her condition, starry-eyed about starting life over in Walnut River with a man she believed would be there for her. One disdainful look from Elizabeth Albright had crushed those dreams. She hated sharing a name with them, but it was Janie's too and she wouldn't deprive her of that.

David stared at her for several moments. "Who picked out Janie's name? You?"

Where did that come from? "Yes. Why?"

"You never said that Joe had had a sister. And from what I learned, he wasn't the type to name his child after her."

It felt as if he'd knocked the air from her lungs. Joe had told her about Jane when they'd first met. The pain of loss in his eyes was what she'd fallen in love with because he'd seemed so caring about his sister who'd died. Courtney had bonded with him over the hardships of their pasts and he'd made a fool of her. The bitterness of that burned through her.

She lifted her chin and looked at David. "There was no reason for me to tell you that. Obviously the Albrights felt the need to share."

"Actually, they took the blame for his behavior."

What was he trying to tell her? "The dots are there, but you've got to connect them for me."

"They told me about losing their daughter in the context of explaining how their son became a selfish, self-centered, manipulative hustler."

Suddenly Courtney felt as if her legs wouldn't hold her up.

She rested against the arm of the sofa. "I'm surprised they acknowledged Joe's problems."

The Albrights had admitted as much to him, but not to her. Then the truth hit her. David was their equal, but she was nothing more than a hustler by association, an opportunist who would never rise above her shabby background. What they hadn't counted on was her determination to overcome the past and be gum on their shoes, an annoyance—someone they couldn't get rid of easily.

"They're not bad people, Court. Life kicked them around and they handled it the best way they knew how. After losing their child, they tried to pick up the pieces, but tragedies affect the whole family—including the healthy, surviving child. They cared enough about Joe to let him stand on his own because Jane's traumatic illness caused him to get lost in the shuffle—"

"Don't you dare defend him to me," she said hotly.

"I'm not. It's just that I have an idea why he turned out like he did."

"He voluntarily walked away from the opportunity to have a relationship with his child. Are you telling me you can understand that?"

"That's indefensible. I'd never turn my back on the people I care about."

"But you did, David."

"What?" His blue eyes went cold as ice.

"Your father talked about you all the time. He'd come in the gift shop and chat, ask about Janie. I'd tell him stories and he'd remember you at the same age. He loved you and needed you. Where were you all those years? Tell me how that's different from Joe."

A muscle jerked in his jaw. "My father had a life and could take care of himself. Unlike you and Janie counting on Joe."

He had her there, but she'd hit a nerve. Part of her was glad. She could only blame her harshness on the ever-present fight-or-flight mentality she'd known for as long as she could remember. Flight wasn't an option. She had roots here and wouldn't give them up. The men she'd let into her life had let her down, but Walnut River never had. Her only choice was to fight. But David didn't deserve to be her target.

She stood and started to put her hand on his arm, then curled her fingers into her palm. "I'm sorry, David. That was uncalled for."

"No harm, no foul." He shrugged.

"The thing is, I *can* take care of myself and my daughter. I don't need help from anyone and certainly not the Al-brights."

"Understood."

"I appreciate everything you've done."

She was walking a fine line and the edge was starting to cut her and Janie. The little girl talked nonstop about Dr. David this and Dr. David that. She was falling for him and didn't have the reserves of worldly wisdom to keep out the hurt when he walked away. Her little girl believed in fairy tales and happy endings and it was up to Courtney to protect her.

"It's no big deal." David walked to the door and grabbed his jacket from the hook beside it. "I'll see you, Court."

When he was gone she felt lower than a snake's belly in the deepest place on the planet. He'd only been trying to help, but old habits died hard. And because they did, she had to wonder what he got out of helping her.

On a whim, she booted up her computer tucked away on a small desk in the corner of the living room. When she'd logged onto the Internet, she typed in *David Wilder, M.D.,*

Plastic Surgeon, and a ton of stuff popped up. *Stunned* didn't begin to describe how she felt when she read about him.

The information should have been reassuring. Instead it made her afraid because all her defensive shields lowered in a heartbeat.

Chapter Eight

Courtney always manned—or was it womaned—the cash register at the hospital's gift shop when her staff was on a break. That was the case the next day when Dr. Peter Wilder walked in. She'd always thought him a good-looking man and still did. But she couldn't help making comparisons between the brothers and every time it was thoughts of David that made her pulse race. That condition had worsened after what she'd learned on the Internet.

"Hi, Courtney. How are you?"

She held up her injured arm. "On the mend, thanks."

"And Janie? How's she doing?"

"David—Dr. Wilder—"

Peter grinned. "I know who he is."

"Right." She brushed a strand of hair behind her ear. "He took out the stitches in her chin and that's healing nicely. To fix her cheek will require another surgery in about three weeks. Or less."

He nodded. "Check with Human Resources. You may be eligible for programs through the hospital to help with the expenses."

"Thanks for the tip. I'll do that." Apparently being a hero was a family trait. Their father had passed it down to both of his sons. "In fact, I'm glad you stopped in so I could thank you personally."

"For?"

"Bringing David in to look at Janie."

"Ella made the call."

"Then it was a joint effort. He's going to do the repair right here at Walnut River General. He assures me that except for her dimple, he can make her look just like she did before the accident."

She wished someone had warned her that David was one of the good guys before she'd revealed her snarky streak. According to what she'd read about him, he elevated benevolence and compassion to an art form.

"So he's coming back for the surgery?" Peter asked.

"Actually, he's taking time off and staying until the procedure," Courtney confirmed.

"That's news to me." Peter leaned against the counter. "I wonder what he's been doing with himself."

"Spending time with my daughter, for one thing," she said. "Janie couldn't go to school and I had to work. David offered to help out and keep her company."

"What a guy." Peter's dark eyebrows pulled together in a puzzled expression.

"Is that different from when you knew him? I—I mean growing up together?"

He thought for a moment, then said, "That's tough to answer. We haven't spent a lot of time together as grown men. I just remember that Dad always said David was the one who turned his hair white." He picked up a roll of mints and set them on the glass counter. "Is there any reason in particular you're wondering about David?"

So many reasons, so little time. Mostly she wanted to know because any piece of information that would help her keep David Wilder at arm's length would be greatly appreciated. She was hoping Peter would tell her that what she'd seen on the Internet about David fixing poor kids' faces was all about PR that would bring rich women to his office in droves. Somehow she wanted his brother to spin the good deeds into something that would crush the crush that got a little bigger every time she saw David.

"I looked David up on the Internet," she said.

"Checking out his credentials before he does Janie's procedure?" Peter teased.

"Something like that," she hedged. "The thing is, I found a lot of information on his work in third-world countries."

"I never heard Beverly Hills described that way before."

Courtney blinked. He had to be teasing. "No, I meant his trips to other countries. When he does surgery on impoverished kids with little or no access to medical care. The before and after pictures on the Net were pretty remarkable. Some of the children had incredible traumas or deformities and David performed miracles."

Peter straightened and stared down at her. "What are you talking about?"

"He's like the Indiana Jones of the medical community." She stared at him. "You don't know about this?"

"Not a clue."

"He never told you about these trips?" She needed to clarify, make sure they were on the same page.

"Not a word."

"Why?"

"I couldn't tell you." Peter ran his fingers through his hair. "Since he left home David hasn't been in touch regularly.

Something happened. A falling out with Dad. He wouldn't talk about it and as far as I know they never spoke before my father passed away."

Courtney felt a deep sadness for David and his father. James Wilder was probably the finest man she'd ever known and she'd have given anything if he'd been her father instead of the one fate had burdened her with. What had caused David and his dad to part ways? Why did he give of his time and skill to strangers yet drift away from his own family?

As a mother she could imagine the incredible pain and anguish if Janie turned away from her. She couldn't stand it if her daughter wasn't in her life. And she hoped she would always be that important to her child.

She met Peter's gaze. "It's not like he was trying to hide anything. It was all there on the Internet."

"Yeah. But he's my brother. Who knew I'd need the Internet to find out what he's been up to?"

"I'm sorry. I don't know what to say."

"That makes two of us. But David has some explaining to do." He took a bill out of his pocket, indicating he wanted to pay for his purchase.

Courtney ran the roll of mints across the scanner and gave him change for a twenty. "I'm glad I got a chance to say thanks for your help after the accident."

"Don't mention it. I appreciate the 411 on my brother. You can bet I want to know more about it."

That made two of them. While she watched Peter walk out of the gift shop a surreal feeling washed over her. Usually if something seemed too good to be true, it was. Not David. He turned out to be better than he looked. And he looked pretty darn good.

So, where did that leave her? With more questions than answers. She wanted answers because this was the man who was going to fix her little girl. Mostly that's why she wanted to know him. At least that's what she tried to believe. Because if he was really as good as he looked on paper, she didn't have a prayer of getting her heart through this unscathed.

Time off was a good opportunity to catch up on his professional reading. With a stack of medical journals beside him on the table, David sat in one of the wing chairs in his room at the Walnut River Inn. Dinner had consisted of an excellent Cornish game hen with all the trimmings served in the inn's huge, but homey, yellow-and-red gingham kitchen. He'd sat by himself at one of the tables for four.

This wasn't how he normally spent a Saturday night. At home it usually started with a movie or play followed by dinner at a trendy, expensive restaurant with a hot blonde, brunette or redhead across the table from him and hotter sex back at his place. For reasons he couldn't explain, he didn't miss it. The hot ladies, not the sex. That he missed quite a bit.

A vision of Courtney flashed into his mind, her lips wet and swollen from his kiss, her smoky eyes locked on his. Need slammed him like a sledgehammer to the chest. And how freaking stupid was that? The last time he'd seen her, she'd basically taken him to task for messing with her life. Where did he get this weakness for damsels in distress? She needed his skill as a doctor, but nothing else. And damned if that didn't make him *want* something else. Is that what had happened to him in college? Had he really learned nothing from that nightmare?

His thoughts went straight back to that time and the intensity of his desire to help the woman he'd thought he loved. When she'd got what she wanted and the manure had hit the fan, she'd dropped him like a hot rock. Once Janie's surgery was over, Courtney wouldn't need him. So, thinking about her like this was an exercise in futility. Or insanity. Or both.

A knock on the door saved him the trouble of deciding which. After setting his reading material on the table beside him, he crossed the room and opened the door.

"Courtney?"

"Hi, David. I hope I'm not disturbing you."

That was up for debate. Which was more disturbing? Thoughts of her driving him crazy or Courtney in person doing the same thing? He couldn't decide which form of self-torture was worse.

"Nope. Just reading." He opened the door wider. "Do you want to come in? We could go in the inn's living room—"

As voices of the other guests drifted to them, she shook her head. "No. Here is fine. I'd like to talk to you if that's okay."

More than okay, based on this feeling of being too happy to see her. "Sure," he said casually, standing back, then shutting the door behind her. "Where's Janie?"

"Spending the night at her friend's house. Melanie," she added, nervously twisting her fingers together. "Mel's mom is a nurse at the hospital and said she'd make sure the girls took it easy. No rough stuff. DVDs and dolls. Nothing more strenuous than that."

She was babbling, David noticed. And Courtney wasn't a babbler. So what was she nervous about?

"Have a seat," he said, indicating the matching wing chairs in the cozy alcove across from the four-poster bed.

"Thanks." She put her purse on the floor beside her.

"May I take your coat?" Subtext of the question was whether or not she'd be staying a while, and he hoped the answer was yes.

"Thanks again," she said, shrugging out of the fleece-lined windbreaker.

He settled it on the doorknob, then sat in the open chair beside her. "So, what brings you here? Now that I think about it, how'd you get in?"

"I know Greta Sanford and her husband. I took a history class from Mr. Sanford. He teaches college part time in Pittsfield and helps with the inn. So he can vouch that I'm not a serial killer."

"Good to know. So— What's up?" He rested his elbows on his knees.

"I looked you up on the Internet."

"I'm flattered."

"I didn't do it because I have a crush on you." And yet a blush crept into her cheeks.

"Okay."

"It was because I didn't trust you."

"So you do think *I'm* a serial killer," he teased.

"God, no." Her gaze jumped to his. "But you're too good to be true. That's not normal."

Maybe in her world, from what little she'd told him. The thought made him want to pull her into his arms and shelter her from everything bad. But he didn't and the self-torture ratcheted up.

"How do you mean *not normal?*" he asked.

"You know—if it walks like a duck, quacks like a duck—"

"It must be a duck. Yeah, I get that, but—" He shook his head. "I'm lying. I don't get that."

"You're a plastic surgeon. You look like a movie star. But—"

"Have I ever told you how much I hate the word *plastic?*"

Her mouth turned up at the corners. "But you're a really nice guy. I just wanted to know more about you."

"And did you find anything to change your mind? Prove I'm not a duck?"

"No. That is, you're not a duck. I found out about your trips to Africa and Central America to help kids with facial deformities. I saw the photographs of what you do and under what conditions. The thing is—"

"Yes?" he prodded when she hesitated.

"I mentioned this to your brother and he didn't know about it. Why would you not say anything to your family about the wonderful work you do?"

The subtext of her question was—what do you get out of it? He wanted to say "nothing" because thinking about his motives brought back all the bad stuff. But he wanted to be honest with her. Maybe because men had let her down on a regular basis and he didn't want to be one more on the infamous list. To answer her question, he needed to explain what had happened between him and his father. It seemed right finally to tell someone. It felt right to tell her.

"I don't broadcast it because somehow publicity and praise cancel out the lesson."

She inched forward on her chair in order to see his face without the lamp in the way. "What lesson?"

He stood and ran his fingers through his hair. "In college— There was a girl—"

"Your father didn't approve of her?"

Interesting she would go there. "No. Actually, they never met. His disapproval came after he was notified by the college when I was caught with answers for an exam."

"David—" She stood and looked up at him, questions swirling in her big, brown eyes.

"Not for me. They were for her." He held up his hand. "Stupid, I know. Don't ask."

She studied him intently, then nodded. "Okay. What happened?"

"I got thrown out of school."

"So— What? You're not really a doctor? You're the great imposter?"

"If there was any upside, it was that I only lost a year. I couldn't transfer my credits so I started from scratch at another school on the west coast. As far from my father and

Walnut River as I could get." He shrugged, not wanting to share the stupid, painful details. "What doesn't kill you makes you stronger. Starving student. Pick your cliché, although the starving part wasn't too far off the mark in my case."

"So you made it on your own."

He nodded. "In my residency I was mentored by a prestigious group of plastic—reconstructive—surgeons in Beverly Hills. Then they invited me to join the practice. They were approached by an international children's health care organization to have a doctor in the group volunteer a week in Central America doing surgeries on kids with cleft palates, facial trauma, burns, minimizing scars. I drew the short straw."

"Why the short straw? I found articles about your regular trips to other countries. It doesn't sound like you hated it."

"Yeah." He saw the look in her eyes, the doubt and skepticism. "Before you ask what I get out of it, let me just say the gratitude of those parents was payment enough. Some of them didn't speak English. There were translators, but the words didn't matter. God, they so didn't matter." He drew in a shuddering breath as he struggled to find the words to explain the power of the experience.

"Nothing mattered except the concern in their eyes for their children. And the soul-deep appreciation in their expressions. Word spread and people brought their kids to me to be fixed. I could see in their faces that they'd lost hope of a decent, normal life for their child. But if there was a single chance—" He held up his hands. "With these, I gave them back their hope. I changed lives for the better. I found out what my father meant."

"About what? What did he say?"

"He told me I would never appreciate the blessings I'd been born with until I learned to give back and not just take. He was right, Courtney." He rubbed the back of his neck.

"No, David. Obviously he was angry."

"Yeah. But it was more than that. Even then I was a good study of faces. I saw how much I'd let him down." He shook his head, remembering the desolate expression in James Wilder's eyes, the same eyes that stared back at him from the mirror every day. "In so many ways I disappointed him—" Emotion clogged his throat, he stopped and turned away.

"He loved you, David—" She put her hand on his back.

"I don't know any more."

The warmth of Courtney's fingers on his back burned straight into him, to a place he'd closed off so long ago. Something about her drew him in, lit a candle inside him, made him want to be close to her.

Needing to see her, he turned back. Courtney's eyes swam with sympathy just before she put her arms around him. He pulled her closer and buried his face in her sweet-smelling hair.

"David—"

He heard the need in her voice, recognized it as an echo of his own. Every thought went out of his head but one. If he didn't kiss her right now, his soul would dry up and blow away.

Courtney stared at him and braced for impact when his eyes darkened and his body tensed, urging her subtly closer to him. But nothing could prepare her for the heat, and, just like that, she was swept away, clinging to him as her safe harbor in the eye of the storm.

He tunneled his fingers into her hair and pressed the back of her head gently, making the contact of their mouths firmer, deeper, stronger. His breathing was fast and uneven. They were pressed together from chest to thigh, nearly as close as two people could get, making it impossible for her to ignore his erection pressing against her belly.

David eased his mouth from hers and stared into her eyes for several moments. The naked need in his gaze took her breath away and underscored his self-control when he gently kissed the tip of her nose.

He smiled. "I guess there's no point in lying about it. I want you. And the ball, as they say, is in your court."

Exhilaration speared through the sultry blast of heat holding her in its grip. He was turned on. She'd got his motor running. There'd been no one for her since Joe, and he hadn't wanted her after she'd told him she was pregnant, not even when he was home on leave. Courtney had forgotten what it felt like for a man to want her and to want him right back.

Could she turn off her head and simply let nature take its course? Worry about everything else later? For now she longed to just give in to the needs pouring through her body.

"Court?" His gaze moved over her face, studying her. "You're thinking. I don't like it when you think too much."

"Sorry. That's just me being me."

"What's going through your mind?"

"Not much, because I'm pretty sure all the circuits are shorted out. What I know is more instinct."

"Okay," he said warily. "What do you know?"

"I need you to touch me. Somewhere. Anywhere. I need to feel your hands on my skin."

He grinned and turned up the heat. "I can do that."

He put his hands at her waist and slid his palms beneath her sweater, up her sides, stopping when he brushed his thumbs over her nipples. The light touch produced a surge of electricity so strong it fried any brain circuits that might have survived his initial assault on her mouth. A shudder coursed through her body and the heavenly sensation made her mouth open and her eyes drift shut.

"Lady," he said, his voice husky with need, "when you look like that, it's all I can do not to throw you on the bed and ravish you."

She looked at him and smiled. "What's stopping you?"

He hesitated a heartbeat before saying, "Not a damn thing."

He yanked back the comforter and sheets and backed her up against the mattress, kissed her hard, then said, "Hold that thought."

He disappeared and a light in the bathroom flashed on for a moment. Then he returned holding a square packet and set it on the nightstand. Courtney was so far gone she hadn't even thought about protection. She didn't care why he had it; she was just grateful that he did.

Without words he slid his arms around her. His mouth captured hers, tasting of humor and hunger and heat. As his teeth grazed her bottom lip, she felt his hands at her waist, unbuttoning her jeans before sliding down the zipper and skimming the denim to her hips. She toed off her sneakers and let him draw the cloth over her knees and to the floor. When she had stepped out of the pants, he took the bottom of her sweater in his fingers and gently pulled it up and over her head.

Her left sleeve caught on her cast and he tenderly freed it before gently kissing each of her fingertips. As he unhooked her bra, she undid the buttons on his shirt and pressed her palm to his bare flesh. It was warm and appealingly masculine and soft, except for the sprinkling of hair across his chest.

While she was spinning in the headiness of the moment, he was busy removing shoes, pants and shirt. Just like that it was a level playing field, with both of them naked as the day they were born. Instead of embarrassment, Courtney reveled in his awed expression as he openly looked her over from head to toe.

He touched the colorful healing bruise on her shoulder, where the seatbelt had pulled tight in the accident. "Does it hurt?"

She shook her head. "Not unless you're talking vanity. Yellow does nothing for my skin tone."

Lowering his head, he kissed the mark. "You have incredibly beautiful skin," he murmured.

"Ah, flattery from the renowned reconstructive surgeon, Dr. David Wilder."

"I'm not trying to sweet-talk you, Court. That was a sincere compliment."

His vulnerable side was showing and it effectively lowered her defenses.

"I know. I'm nervous, David." She fixed her gaze on the center of his chest. "Gossip has you being with some of the most beautiful women in the world. And I'm just me. Battered and broken. On top of that I haven't done this for a really long time. I'm probably going to mess this up. It's a talent of mine—"

He touched a finger to her lips. "Stop thinking. More important, stop talking. Trust me."

Of the three, trust was the most difficult.

He lifted her into his arms, snuggling her to his chest. Her heart hammered against his, matching him beat for beat. Settling her in the center of the big, soft mattress, he slid beside her and touched his lips to hers again, effectively shutting down brain function.

When she opened her mouth, he didn't hesitate to accept the invitation and slid his tongue inside. As he stroked and sucked, liquid heat and pounding need pooled in her belly. He nipped her lower lip with his teeth as he kissed his way down her neck, over her chest and took her breast in his mouth. The soft, erotic touch coursed through her and she felt as if she were on fire.

That was nothing compared to the feeling of his hand inching down her belly before his fingers parted the curls between her thighs to slide inside her. She was wet and ready and nearly mindless with wanting.

"David, please," she whispered.

"In a minute."

Sixty seconds too long, she thought, writhing beneath his oh-so-focused attention. With his thumb, he rubbed the nub where all her nerve endings joined at the center of her femininity. Her breathing was shallow and uneven and she couldn't seem to get enough air into her lungs. The touch was simply too exquisite and she shattered into a million pieces, dissolving into all the colors of the rainbow.

"Oh, David," she said when she could speak. Her still-labored breathing was not conducive to conversation. "That was amazing— But you didn't—"

"I will."

He reached for the condom, opened the packet and slid the sheath on. Then he settled over her, bracing himself on his forearms as he stared, as if he couldn't look at her hard enough.

"That put some color into your cheeks," he said, sliding inside her.

She hooked her legs around his waist. "Let me return the favor."

His eyes darkened to navy blue, then his mouth claimed hers for an exquisitely sweet kiss. He started to move in and out, slowly. But in less time than it took a heart to beat he increased the rhythm. She gave herself over to it, losing herself in the texture and taste of his lips, the sensations of her body humming and her pulse pounding. And the sheer bliss of being with this man. Then he tensed and groaned, his face all angles, shadows, concentration. And intense pleasure.

Several moments later, he kissed her softly, then rested his forehead against hers. "For the record, the way you messed that up?" He blew out a long breath, then grinned the grin that rocked her world. "It really worked for me."

She laughed. "Me, too."

He rolled to the side and off the bed. "Don't move. I'll be right back."

She didn't have to move to start thinking again. Passion was satisfied. Doubts filled the void when need receded. She hated the doubts. But she'd learned life would bite her in the backside if she ignored them.

Chapter Nine

When David walked out of the bathroom, Courtney was putting her shoes on. "So much for doctor's orders not to move."

She looked up and straightened in the chair. Her gaze was locked on his face, which reminded him he was the only one in the room still naked. Her tense expression was a dead giveaway that the post-coital glow had dimmed.

He walked past her and, reaching into the drawer beneath the entertainment center, pulled out a pair of sweats, then stepped into them. "What's wrong, Court?"

"Nothing. I have to go."

"What's your hurry?"

"I need to get home. Janie—"

"Is spending the night with a friend," he reminded her.

"I guess I mentioned that." She twisted her fingers nervously.

"Yeah, you did. Which makes me wonder if there's something wrong."

"I just feel like I need to be home."

He folded his arms over his bare chest and had the satisfaction of watching her eyes darken as her gaze was drawn there. "So this isn't about running away."

"Of course not. I'm a responsible mother. Unlike my own," she added. "Scratch that. Ancient history."

"Right. A shrink could have a field day with that slip of the tongue."

David wasn't sure why he didn't just say adios, but something wouldn't let him back off. One minute Courtney was smiling, the next she was skidding straight into escape mode. What the hell had happened?

"What do you want me to say?" Courtney asked.

"We just had sex, and it was mind-blowingly good if I do say so myself. Now you're setting a land speed record for home and talking about your mother. What's up with that, Court?"

Her chin edged up, proud and independent. "I'm not like my mother."

"I never said you were."

"No, this is me saying I'm not like her. Trying to believe I'm not like her. This—" She swung out an arm, indicating the room, "This isn't like me at all. I don't sleep with men I've only known a short time."

He couldn't help thinking it had something to do with thanking him. She was strapped for cash and would be grateful to anyone who could do for her daughter what he could. It was an ugly thought and one he kept to himself.

Instead he asked, "Was that your mother's pattern?"

"She didn't stick around long enough for me to make inquiries." There was an edge of bitterness to her voice. "But in his drunken babbling, my father mentioned it a time or two."

"So why did you come here?" he asked.

"I wanted to ask you about the information on the Internet," she defended. "Because it didn't make sense that no one knew about your good deeds. I didn't come here to sleep with you."

"Do you mind if I ask why you did? Sleep with me, I mean."

"Bruised ego, doctor?" One corner of her full mouth curved up.

"Maybe. Mostly just curious. Why did you go to bed with me?"

Tension highlighted a haunted sort of pain in her eyes. "I thought I was going to die in that accident. When you go through something like that it changes you. Makes you painfully aware of regrets, the path not taken. You always believe there's time."

There was a lot of that going around. It had always been his intention to get in touch with his father and reconnect, put the past behind them. Now he never could. "Yeah. I know what you mean."

"I'm attracted to you." She laughed but it wasn't a carefree sound. "I guess I wanted to take the path. Just to see."

"And?"

"At the risk of resuscitating your ego—it was great." A blush put roses in her cheeks. "You already knew that."

"I sense a 'but' coming."

"It can't happen again," she said firmly.

"Because you're trying to live down your mother's reputation?"

"I'd like to avoid any comparison."

David wanted to wrap her in his arms, but for once listened to the warning that women in need were trouble. Besides, she looked brittle, as if she might shatter at the slightest touch. "Anyone can see you're an amazing mother. You don't have to prove anything to anyone."

"Except myself. I love my child more than anything in the world. And I'd do anything to protect her, keep her safe and not let her get hurt."

As she caught her top lip between her teeth, David saw the lingering effects of his kisses in her swollen lips. Her eyes were shadowed and her hair tousled from his running his fingers through it. His gut tightened in need and the intense reaction was as swift as it was unexpected. Moments ago he'd been so sure she was out of his system. Clearly he'd been wrong because he wanted her again. Which is exactly why he should let her go.

But he couldn't. She was carrying around a lot of baggage thanks to the men who should have taken care of her and lumping him in with the lowlifes. That bothered him.

"No one is disputing your devotion to Janie," he said.

"Good. Because she's my heart and that means she's at the heart of everything I do."

"So, even though she's not home and you have a cell phone in case she needs you, you feel required to be there?"

"I'm handling this badly." She shook her head. "I had a conversation with Janie just before she went to her friend's. She wanted to know if you have any kids."

"No."

"You're talking biological. The truth is you've got children all over the world. Every one you saved carries a part of you forever."

David was quiet for a moment. "I never thought about it like that."

"You should. Along with other things."

"Like what?" he asked.

"Like the fact that my daughter doesn't remember her father, so as far as she's concerned she's never had one. Until you."

"Me?" Like his wanting Courtney, that came out of nowhere. He'd gone from doctor to daddy?

She rubbed her temples and blew out a breath. "That didn't come out right. Since I'm not getting this accurate by beating around the bush in an attempt to be diplomatic, let me say it straight out. Janie wants a father. You're her hero for fixing her face and you pay attention to her. Everything she wants."

He ran his fingers through his hair. "Her standards aren't so high, are they?"

"What do you expect? She's six."

"I see what you mean. Do you want me to talk to her?" he suggested.

She shook her head. "Don't for one second think that I don't appreciate your kindness to my daughter. But I want you to stop spending time with her. David, we both know your life isn't here in Walnut River. We're adults. We understand the ramifications. But Janie doesn't. In her mind she's writing her own happily-ever-after where you chuck a lucrative medical practice and lavish lifestyle to stay here. If she gets too attached to you, it will break her heart when you go. I know what that feels like." She held up her hand. "I'm not an idiot with my head buried in the sand. I stopped doing that because it leaves other parts exposed, if you get my drift. I know sooner or later she'll be hurt—a crush that doesn't work out, misplaced trust in a friend. But this is one of the times I can do something to protect her. If I didn't, what kind of mother would I be?"

David didn't know what to say. He *was* leaving. There'd never been any question about that and he'd never deceived her. So why did he feel the urge to defend himself? Maybe because of all the men who came before him and crushed her dreams. He wanted her to know he wasn't like them. He wanted her in his bed with no promises, no strings attached, no regrets and no looking back. And if he said as much to her, she'd figure it was payback for his help. What he got out of it. His agenda. It was what he'd been after all along. So he said nothing.

As the silence stretched out, he watched Courtney's face and the expectant expression that faded to one of resignation followed swiftly by disappointment. It was as though the light went out of her. Her full mouth pulled into a straight line and she brushed past him to retrieve her coat from the doorknob.

"I'll just be going," she said.

"So this is all about protecting Janie?"

"Yes." She slid her arms into the sleeves.

He moved closer and lifted her hair free and over the collar, then pulled the sides together at her throat. "Are you sure?"

"What are you asking?"

"You're not running away to protect yourself?"

"I'm not saying you're right about that, but it makes good sense, given the fact that you didn't really try very hard to talk me out of it. Goodbye, David." She opened the door, then softly closed it behind her.

David blew out a long breath as he stared at where she'd been standing. For a small woman, she'd sure managed to fill up this room, and it felt pretty empty now.

He was going to try like hell not to see the biggest and most expensive room at the Walnut River Inn as a metaphor for his life.

At work bright and early Monday morning, Courtney breathed a sigh of relief that Janie had gone back to school. Soon the surgery on her face would be behind them and so would David. Something just this side of pain tightened in her chest. It had been her idea to put distance between them, but she found herself wishing that he'd tried harder to convince her she was wrong.

Probably she'd headed off trouble and that was a good thing. Slowly but surely things were getting back to normal. A vision of being in his arms flashed through her mind and she realized nothing would ever be normal again.

As soon as the thought was there, she shut it down. She'd lived in the moment. She'd wanted to be with him and couldn't make herself say no. Part of surviving an accident such as she'd had was a clearer, deeper appreciation of life. It was permission to live fully. No regrets. Probably. Maybe.

After counting out change for the cash register and making sure the shelves were neatly and fully stocked, promptly at 9:00 A.M. she unlocked and opened the gift-shop doors.

Behind the glass counter, she checked over her list of inventory and made notes for her monthly order. At ten she had an appointment with a woman who hand-crocheted baby blankets, afghans, hats and gloves, and who wanted to display her items in the shop. Courtney thought the idea had potential. She had the nurses on the floors let her know when a patient didn't get visitors and made it a point to send up a balloon bouquet or something cheery, and a cozy, handmade lap blanket could bring a bit of comfort and a sense of home. There was nothing happier than a baby being born and visitors were always looking for a special gift.

When she heard footsteps, she looked up. "Hi, Ella."

"Hi, yourself." The doctor was wearing blue scrubs under a white lab coat which meant a rotation in the E.R. today.

"How are you?"

"Never better."

Courtney figured as much. The woman still glowed so brightly she needed a lead shield for radioactive containment. "That's good to hear. What can I do for you?"

"I need a card," she said.

"All along that wall." Courtney pointed with her left hand. The green cast caught Ella's attention. "How's the wrist?"

"I'd say never better," she commented wryly, "but it was better before I broke it. Now I can tell you it doesn't hurt, but it itches like crazy."

Ella nodded with satisfaction. "As it should."

"We can put a man on the moon, float a space station and

send ships there to supply it. Wouldn't you think someone could invent a cast that doesn't itch?"

"Sometimes there's no substitute for the tried and true."

"If it ain't broke, don't fix it?" Courtney said smiling.

"Yeah." Ella stuck her hands in the pockets of her lab coat. "How's Janie doing?"

"Back to school."

"That's good news."

"Yeah." It meant she didn't have to see David when she got home from work. Janie had said she wanted to call his cell and invite him to dinner. Courtney had managed to talk her out of that with a lot of verbal tap dancing and a heartfelt plea to wait and see how she tolerated getting back into her regular routine. "I left instructions with the school staff that if she got too tired or complained of anything more than a hangnail, they should call me."

Ella nodded. "Kids are so resilient. They bounce back pretty quickly."

"Thank God."

"I'm sure you know this, Courtney, but the accident wasn't your fault."

David had told her the same thing. Thinking of him made her heart stutter and her stomach flutter. "I appreciate you saying that."

"I'm not patronizing you. The road was icy. You didn't do it on purpose, that's why they're called accidents. Otherwise they'd be known as deliberates."

Courtney smiled. What was it about the Wilder clan that could make her smile when it was the last thing she wanted to do? David did that to her all the time. He'd been a light in the darkness during this horrible time. Now she knew he was a light in the darkness for a lot of people all over the world. Now she knew he had no agenda for helping her except maybe personal demons of his own. Somehow that got to her more than his looks and personality. He wasn't perfect. It made him human. Like her.

"Thanks for saying that," she said.

Ella nodded. "It's the truth. Give yourself a break. Get off the guiltmobile."

"I'll try."

"Okay. I'm stopping the Ella Wilder lecture tour. At least long enough to pick out my card."

"Let me know if I can help you with anything."

"Will do."

Courtney looked down at her paperwork, but concentration was elusive. David's siblings both worked at Walnut River General, which meant that as long as she had a job here she was going to see them. Every time she did, she'd think of him. How could she help it? There was a resemblance in looks and personality. She'd have been better off not meeting David Wilder, but Janie wouldn't have. And so she bought a ticket for another ride on the guiltmobile.

Ella came to the counter and handed her several cards. "Thanks to the Internet, the fine art of note- and letter-writing is dying out. Because I'm busy like everyone else, this is my way of putting it on life support."

Courtney rang up the purchases, took Ella's twenty-dollar bill and handed her her change, then put the cards in a small plastic bag. "There you go."

"Thanks." She stuck the bag in her lab coat and started to turn away, then stopped. "I heard about David's trips to developing countries to help the children. You were the one who ratted him out to Peter."

"Yeah." Courtney's cheeks felt hot, as if she'd been caught doing a drive-by. In this technological age, the Internet was a way to cruise past the cute guy's house without getting caught peeking. Usually.

"I often think about David and wonder what he's up to,

but it never occurred to me to look him up on the Web." She frowned. "We were so close growing up, but everything changed after David went to college."

Courtney knew why, but it wasn't her place to say. She'd done enough meddling. If she'd minded her own business, she'd never have learned about his unselfish side. Ignorance of it would have kept her from going to see him, which would have kept her from…sleeping with him. Every time her mind turned a corner there was another memory to make her blush.

"Your brother is a very nice man," Courtney said.

"He is." One eyebrow rose in what looked very much like an aha expression. "So, the rumors are true."

"Rumors?" Courtney went still. "What would those be?"

"It's come to my attention that you and David are spending a lot of time together."

"A lot of time is probably an exaggeration. Because he's Janie's doctor we've seen him. And he offered to stay with her when I came back to work."

"I see."

"One good deed and all that. He stayed for dinner a few times." She shrugged. "But it's nothing personal."

Although sex was about as personal as you could get. But that was nothing more than a weak moment and wouldn't happen again. It was on the tip of her tongue to say so. Then she stopped herself. There was no reason to assure Ella that her intentions toward David were strictly honorable. She had no intentions toward the man.

Still, she tensed. Growing up she'd carried the label of the town drunk's daughter. She'd get glances that held everything from pity to distaste, as if she was not good enough, as if the disgrace of her family background was contagious or would rub off. It was a good thing she'd had school and work to keep her busy or she'd have had a lot of time to feel sorry for herself because no one would let their kids be her friend.

Going to college had been like wiping her slate clean. No one knew about her past until she'd trusted Joe enough to share it. He'd lulled her into a false sense of security, then pulled the rug out from under her when he'd brought her home to meet his folks. That had been a disaster and she'd kicked herself for letting her guard down. It wouldn't happen again.

"Nothing personal?" Ella studied her. "Then you have to tell me how you keep your skin so flawless."

Courtney blinked. "Excuse me?"

"Love is good for the complexion. Right? Yours is glowing—at least it is when you talk about David."

Ella had always been friendly, but Courtney still tensed, waiting for the warning to stay away from her brother. "There's really nothing between me and David."

"Well, darn." Ella sighed. "I was hoping there was something to talk about."

"You were?"

"Big-time. Tell me I'm a selfish witch, but if you and my brother hit it off, we might see more of him."

"His practice is in California."

"There is that. Still, he's drifting, I think. Something's missing in his life and when he decided to stay in Walnut River for a while, I'd hoped he'd find what he was looking for."

"Even if that was me?" Courtney blurted out. She wanted to call the words back but it was too late.

Ella smiled. "You're smart and beautiful. And yet I still like you."

"You do?"

"Why do you sound so surprised? Courtney, you're an inspiration. Single mom raising a terrific kid. I admire you tremendously."

"I—"

"Just say thank you," Ella advised.

"Thank you," Courtney answered automatically.

"I have to go back to work now. See you."

Courtney was too stunned by the words to answer. Dr. Ella Wilder admired her? That was amazing. She'd expected a different reaction. Because David's recent contact with the Albrights had triggered her defensiveness? Everyone else she'd met in Walnut River had accepted and supported her from day one.

That's when she realized that she owned this problem. It was all about attitude. She was so accustomed to being the girl from the wrong side of the tracks, she'd never let herself live on the right side.

She was a decent person trying to be the best person she could be, just like everyone else. The Albrights had rejected her, but that didn't mean she was lacking. It was their problem. And if David hadn't done what he'd done, she might never have seen the difference, had this aha moment.

It was another in a growing list of things to thank him for. Another in a long list of things that could keep him in her heart forever. Janie wasn't the only Albright woman who was falling under his spell.

And she couldn't let it happen.

Chapter Ten

With fifteen minutes to spare, David pulled into the parking lot at the Walnut River Elementary School. The facility was at least fifty years old but had been meticulously maintained. In the front, a flagpole stalwartly flew the Stars and Stripes. Bushes were neatly trimmed and mature maples and sycamores separated the school from Concord Avenue.

He chirped the Beamer's locks, then walked up the familiar path past the administration offices and buildings that housed the upper grades. The primary classes were the farthest from the outside world—whether to protect the most vulnerable or give them fewer distractions, he didn't know.

What he did know was that his chest tightened because it all looked just the same. Janie's first-grade classroom was the exact one he'd gone to.

He stood in the doorway and glanced around. People were just starting to arrive. Instead of the individual desk he'd used there were tables neatly marching the length of the room with two tiny chairs at each. Crayoned and painted artwork was tacked up on boards and strung around the room. The smell of paint and chalk unleashed a flood of memories. Most of them bad. Disappointment was right there at the top of the list. And, although he was pretty sure Courtney would have an issue, he was here because he wouldn't be responsible for a little girl's bad memory.

A woman he assumed was the teacher stood in the front of the room by an adult-sized desk, although she looked small enough to use the kids'. She was giving him a thorough scrutiny and didn't look reassured.

He navigated his way through pint-sized furniture and headed straight for her. "Hi. I should probably introduce myself since I'm crashing this awards ceremony. I'm David Wilder."

"Dr. Wilder." She smiled and the warmth made her look less like the Wicked Witch of the East and more like a kindly fairy godmother. "I'm Carol Hart, Janie's teacher. She's told me all about you."

"Should I be afraid?"

She laughed. "No. It was all good. There's a little hero-worship going on, I think."

"She's a terrific kid."

"Indeed she is. Welcome. It's very nice of you to come."

"She's getting an award. I wouldn't miss it."

She looked past him, then met his gaze. "If you'll excuse me—"

"Of course."

Looking around he noticed the desks had names printed on poster board folded over so it would stand. He found Janie's in the last row. Her seat buddy was Melanie Kier. Probably the friend she'd been visiting the night Courtney had come to see him. He hadn't deliberately kept his humanitarian endeavors a secret, but didn't see any reason to make a big deal out of it. Except, if he'd known Courtney would look at him as though he'd hung the moon, he'd have said something sooner.

Because that was maybe the best and worst night he could remember in a long time. Having her in his arms had been twice as sweet as he'd thought it would be, and he'd imagined it would be pretty sweet. Then she'd gone Jekyll and Hyde on him. One minute warm and soft, the next cool and tough. Warning him against spending too much time with her child because Janie saw him as a substitute father and would be hurt when he went back to his life.

Was it only three days ago? Seemed longer, much longer. He'd liked seeing Courtney every day and spending time with Janie. Maybe coming here was an excuse to see Court. Maybe he was selfish. It wouldn't be the first time and he was paying for that. But this was about a promise and he intended to keep it.

As the hands on the clock closed in on seven, the room filled up with adults and children and the noise level rose accordingly. That didn't drown out Janie's voice when she spotted him.

"Dr. David!"

"Hi, kiddo." He squatted down and she threw her arms around him, her cast scraping his neck.

"You came." The bandage still covered half her face, but the other half was all smiles. "I wasn't sure you would."

"I'm happy to be invited," he said. "It's not every day you get a student-of-the month award."

Courtney put a hand on her daughter's shoulder. "David, I didn't know you'd be here."

"I forgot to tell you. I asked him to come, Mommy." Janie left one arm on his shoulder. "Mrs. Hart said I could."

David stood. "I met your teacher. She's very nice."

"Yes, she is." Courtney's tone was cool, but the pulse at the base of her throat was jumping like crazy.

Janie tugged on his hand. "I have to go, Mommy. I have to sit by Mrs. Hart to get my award."

"Okay, sweetie. I'll be right here. I've got the camera," Courtney said, holding it up.

A few minutes later Mrs. Hart asked for everyone's attention and began the ceremony. There were scholastic achievement medals, citizenship awards and then the all-around student of the month. When Courtney tried to manage the digital camera with one good hand, he took it from her.

"I can do it," she protested.

"I can do it better." He looked down at her. "Height and dexterity."

"Thanks. I appreciate that."

Maybe. But she wasn't happy about him being here. He did his best to ignore the chill as he took pictures and did his level best to get most of them from Janie's good side. When the awards were over, everyone was invited to stay for cookies and juice. Janie was busy visiting with her friends.

Courtney took her camera back and stashed it in her purse. "May I speak to you outside?"

"Sure."

He followed her and they stopped several feet from the door, by an overhang support. An outside light on the wall beside the classroom emphasized the tension in her face. "What's up?"

"I think you know."

"Okay. Yeah. In my defense I have to say that Janie invited me."

"And I explained that spending time with her could generate expectations that you're not prepared or in a position to meet."

"I understand. But I promised her before you made your little speech. Promises trump ultimatums."

"David, I'm not ungrateful for your time. And Janie is beyond excited that you're here. But what about the next time there's an event in her life and you're on the other side of the country? This is just the sort of thing I meant about not getting attached."

"I'll explain—"

"She doesn't really understand anything except that she's getting used to having you around. After her surgery you'll be gone. How is she going to feel then? I'm trying to protect her."

"Me too. Because I showed up she'll remember that I didn't lie to her."

"David, I just don't want her to be let down."

"Neither do I. If anyone knows disappointment, it's me," he said, surprised at the welling of anger and resentment in his voice.

Courtney's eyes widened. "What happened? Who lied to you?" she asked gently.

He let out a long breath as he looked around. "I went to school here. Feels like a million years ago."

"With the dinosaurs. Must have been exciting. You're lucky they didn't have you for lunch," she teased.

"I was pretty fast. They couldn't catch me." Then he turned serious again. "But for everything else, I couldn't catch a break."

"What do you mean?" She folded her arms over her chest. "You've got it all."

"Now. Not then. This was where I learned that bad behavior got my father's attention."

"I don't understand. James Wilder was incredibly generous with his time and interest. He was caring to Janie and me when I was a stranger and didn't know anyone. Why would you, his own son, have to act out for him to notice you?"

"I sound like a spoiled brat, don't I?" He met her gaze. "Now that I'm an adult, and a doctor, I get that he was a busy man. My inner child is okay with that part."

"Then what part is still bugging your inner spoiled brat?"

"The part where he promised to show up for a school function or a soccer or football game and didn't. The part where he put everything and everyone else in the family on hold for Anna."

"Your sister?"

"*Adopted* sister."

"That shouldn't matter."

"It wouldn't," he protested. "If the sacrifice had made a difference. But she's deliberately put distance between herself and the rest of the family. It sounds stupid to say *repay*, no one expects payback for giving her a home. But to turn her back is a slap in the face when Dad bent over backwards at the expense of the rest of his family to make her feel like a Wilder. There are obligations."

"You're not walking in her shoes, David."

He frowned. "What does that mean?"

"Maybe she has a good reason for her behavior. When you had a falling-out with your father, I'm guessing you felt justified in turning your back." When he opened his mouth, she said, "Don't try to tell me you didn't do that. You had a choice. You could have blinked first and contacted him."

She was right. He knew that. Finding a way to live with that regret wouldn't be easy. "What's your point?"

She put her hand on his sleeve. "I'm not trying to hurt you, David. Truly I'm not. Just playing devil's advocate. I'm just pointing out that we all do what we think is best at the time. My father was drinking himself to death and I stayed because he was family and I was obligated. Was it best for me?" She sighed. "Probably not. You struck out on your own and made something remarkable out of your life and career."

"Is that a compliment, Mrs. Albright?"

"Not for you. It's for your inner child. He's got issues." The corners of her mouth turned up. "My point is that we shouldn't judge someone without hearing their side of the story. Maybe Anna is choosing to exercise her free choice and is waiting until she feels sure of herself before committing to the Wilder clan."

"Maybe." He wasn't so sure, but he didn't want her to take her hand off his arm and challenging her would do that. "I didn't mean to go Psych 101 on you."

"It's okay. Nice to know Dr. Perfect has flaws."

"More than you know. But breaking promises isn't one of them." He put his hand over hers. "I never meant to upset you, Court. That's the last thing I'd do."

"I know."

"And my only intention tonight was to give Janie a good memory."

"Thanks for that. It means a lot to her." Courtney's voice thickened with emotion. "We should go back inside. She'll be wondering where we are."

David didn't really know where he was. It was absolutely true that he'd come tonight because of his promise. But if he was being honest with himself, it was all about Courtney. She was constantly on his mind, no matter how hard he fought against it. And now... Looking at her...

In his bed she was pretty memorable. By moonlight she took his breath away. That was bad on more levels than he could count and he could count really high.

"Mommy, I can't sleep."

Courtney glanced up from the computer where she'd just started working on an assignment for her online class. Janie stood in the doorway to the hall.

"Janie, you only went to bed five minutes ago."

"That's a long time."

"Maybe for you, but not for me." Courtney got up and squatted in front of her. "Is anything bothering you?"

The little girl's small fingers plucked at her pink flannel nightgown. "I was thinking about my daddy."

Courtney held in a groan. "Do you want to talk about it?"

She wanted to groan again when Janie nodded. As much as she would have preferred to blow it off and pretend the man had never existed, that wasn't a good idea. It had all the makings of a bad session with Dr. Phil. Janie needed to express her feelings, so that's what they'd do.

"Okay."

"Hot chocolate might help me talk. And sleep," she added.

Courtney suppressed a smile. "Coming right up."

After putting cocoa and milk in two mugs, followed by just the right amount of nuking, the two of them sat side by side on the sofa.

"So what's keeping you awake, baby?"

Janie took a sip. "I was just thinkin'. About my daddy."

"I see." Damn. Damn. Damn. "What about him?"

"Just that I don't 'member much. Can you tell me stuff? About what he was like?"

"He was handsome." Many women had thought so. They'd flirted openly with him and he'd returned the favor. More often than not it didn't stop there.

"What else?"

"He was smart." Smart enough to not get caught when he didn't stop there. Until that last time.

"What did he do in the army?"

Courtney wasn't sure. Their communication had been almost nonexistent after he'd suddenly gone into the army. Because he hadn't discussed the decision, it should have been a clue that they had no relationship. But she was too dense to get the message. She couldn't tell Janie any of that.

"Your father worked hard to make America a safe place for you to grow up."

"Because he loved me?"

"Very much." She hoped that wasn't a lie, but Joe hadn't done much to show whether or not he cared.

"And he loved you."

Fortunately that was stated as a fact and not a question because Courtney's only truthful answer could be that Joe never really loved anyone but himself. Wasn't it supposed to be the good stuff you remembered when someone you'd shared so much with was gone? When she looked back, all she recalled was self-indulgence and manipulation. Even now the hurt lengthened and stretched until it filled every crack in her soul.

She'd shared more with David than she ever had with the man she'd married. The man who had fathered her child. She'd been angry earlier tonight when she'd seen David in Janie's classroom. Angry that he'd ignored her request to keep his distance, but mostly she'd been irritated with herself. Her reaction to seeing him there had been an instantaneous, involuntary spurt of sheer joy that scared the living daylights out of her.

If only she could think of him as the shallow-as-a-cookie-sheet plastic surgeon she'd first believed him to be. But her own snooping had backfired on her. David Wilder was not just a pretty face, there was depth and substance there, too. He'd taken care of her child. He cared about people and actually did something positive because of it. He used his powers for good all over the world.

And the man had a killer sense of humor. If he'd been a toad who had to wear a bag over his head the wit and charm would still have attracted her. She'd known David only a short time, yet a substantial collection of warm memories would remain when he was gone.

How could she sustain a level of anger enough to keep her feelings for him in line? How could she possibly stay mad at a man whose only thought tonight had been to give her baby girl a good memory?

"Melanie thinks Dr. David is a hottie," Janie said.

"Where did Mel hear that kind of language?"

"From her older sister."

"God, help us," Courtney mumbled.

"What?"

"Nothing. Go on."

"Do you think Dr. David is a hottie?"

An honest, straightforward answer to that question could be an entrance exam for admittance to the diplomatic corps. "I think David is very nice-looking."

"Is he your boyfriend?"

"I consider him a friend." A friend with benefits. At least that one time. "And he's a boy." A man, actually, with magic hands that could heal as well as take her to heights she'd never reached before. *Hottie* was definitely the word to describe David.

"Mo-om."

"What?"

Janie finished her hot chocolate, then scooted forward and set the empty cup on the coffee table.

As she looked at her own cast, it crossed Courtney's mind that the two of them were adapting to life with limitations. Probably because they'd had a lot of practice adapting to everything life could throw at them.

"Are you and Dr. David going out?"

Courtney knew what this meant. Some of the nurses with children a little older than Janie joked that their kids were "going out" but never actually went anywhere. They were talking crushes and attraction. She was attracted and would probably get crushed. So how did she answer truthfully?

"David and I have spent a little time together."

"It was a yes-or-no question, Mommy."

Courtney looked down at her child. "Who are you? Perry Mason?"

"Who's that?"

"A famous TV lawyer." She shook her head. "Maybe you should think about law as a career choice when you grow up."

"You're changing the subject," Janie pointed out.

"Yes, I am. Go with it."

"I think Dr. David loves me."

"I'm sure he does, sweetheart." She kissed the top of her daughter's head and snuggled her close. "When you're not grilling me like raw hamburger you're a pretty easy kid to love."

"Mom, I think Dr. David loves you, too."

That was a stunner and made her heart skip a beat or two. "You do? Why?"

"I don't know," she said, shrugging. "I just think he does."

"We've talked about this, sweetie."

Janie sighed. "I know he doesn't live here in Walnut River."

"That's right," Courtney agreed. "He works all the way across the country in California."

"That doesn't mean he can't love us."

"You're right about that."

Though it *would* rule out the traditional family that her little girl was hinting at. Right then and there Courtney's heart shuddered and cracked. She tried so hard to be both mother and father to her child, to give her everything. She still struggled with guilt about the accident and didn't think she'd ever be able to forget the horrific sound of Janie's screams followed by the sound of grinding metal and shattering glass.

There would be financial fallout from the crash that worried her. But this conversation worried her *and* broke her heart. She'd always thought her biggest problem was a tight budget. That was nothing compared to not being able to give her daughter what she wanted most and money couldn't buy: a father, a family.

Courtney couldn't fault her daughter's taste in men. David

would be a fabulous father. And husband? As her one and only attempt had gone horribly wrong, Courtney felt her taste, not to mention her judgment, was questionable at best. Clearly Janie's instincts were better, even though her matchmaking efforts were doomed to failure. Courtney had no illusions that she and David would work out.

Janie frowned. "You got quiet, Mommy. What's wrong?"

"Nothing, sweetie."

"Do you think Dr. David loves you?"

"No."

Make that no way he'd be attracted to someone like her. He'd been linked to some of the world's most beautiful and sophisticated women. Courtney couldn't compete with that even if she wanted to. Which she didn't. The only way to win was not to play.

"I think you're wrong," Janie said on a big yawn.

There was nothing she could say to that because a part of her couldn't help hoping she was wrong, too.

"Come on, little bit, you can't fall asleep here because I don't think I can carry you into bed."

David could. If he was here. The traitorous thought made her just as hopelessly romantic as her daughter. Apparently it was true that the fruit didn't fall far from the tree.

She walked Janie down the hall and tucked her into her impossibly pink bed. Courtney was so tired she wanted to crawl in with her and curl up. It would be a couple of more weeks before Janie's surgery. A couple of more weeks with the potential for a David sighting. More possibilities for her to slide farther down that slippery slope.

Janie was already crushing on him big-time and Courtney wasn't far behind. But one of them had to stay strong enough to get them through when he was gone.

Since Courtney was the grown-up, it was up to her not to fall in love with him.

Chapter Eleven

Courtney was just about to enjoy a cup of tea and fifteen minutes of quiet before Janie came home from her friend's house when there was a knock on the door. She set her steaming mug on the coffee table and went to check. It wasn't often unexpected visitors dropped by and she couldn't help hoping it was David. That night at the school he'd revealed another layer of vulnerability that somehow hiked up the attraction factor for her. As soon as the thought was there she pushed it away. That was dangerous thinking. That was a recipe for disaster.

She peeked through the peephole. That recipe for disaster would be a thousand times better than this; even with the eyepiece distortion she recognized the Albrights. In her opinion, the peephole view was an improvement.

Letting out a long breath, she leaned back against the door and wondered if the fates had it in for her. Between the accident, her and Janie recovering and trying not to make a fool of herself over Dr. Hottie, wasn't life giving her enough challenges? Did karma really feel it necessary to make her face the in-laws who believed she was the spawn of Satan?

It was easier to believe they were the ones with the problem when she didn't have to talk to them. This was all David's fault. Why couldn't he leave well enough alone?

There was another knock and she figured it would be better to get this over with so they'd be gone by the time Janie got home.

She twisted the lock and opened the door and looked from one to the other while her hands shook. "Mrs. Albright. Mr. Albright. This is a surprise."

"Hello, Courtney." Mrs. Albright held herself stiffly and not because of the chilly weather. "We heard about the accident. You're looking well."

"I'm feeling fine. Thanks for asking."

"And…Janie?" Morris asked.

Was there censure in his voice or was her own guilt putting it there? "She's doing remarkably well."

Her mother-in-law unbuttoned her camel-colored cashmere coat. "May we see her?"

"She's at a friend's house."

"I'm sorry to hear that."

The older woman was dressed in a black sweater and coordinating slacks. Courtney had a pretty good idea that the cost of the outfit would supply them with groceries for a month. Or more. This was really awkward and she figured the visit meant only bad stuff. It was on the tip of her tongue to suggest they leave.

Mr. Albright mopped his forehead with a pristine white handkerchief. "May we come in for a moment?"

She'd rather poke herself in the eye with a stick, but what was she supposed to say? "I'm sorry. Of course. Please come in." When the door was closed behind them, she asked politely, "May I take your coats?"

"Thank you." The older man slipped off his overcoat and took his wife's before handing them over.

Courtney hung them on the coat tree beside the door. "Won't you sit down?" She turned back and noticed her mug. "I was just going to have some tea. Would you care for some?"

"No. Thank you," Mrs. Albright answered.

They sat side by side on her home-covered sofa. Reading between the lines of their rigid body language she figured they were thinking this place was tacky times ten. She might not have a lot of money but she had buckets of pride. The rent was paid, there was food on the table and her little girl would never go without while Courtney had breath in her body.

"Charming place." Mrs. Albright's voice was clipped.

"Thanks. We like it."

Mr. Albright drew in a deep breath. "Lots of stairs."

"We like those, too." No matter how hard she tried, she couldn't seem to lose the defensive tone. Why didn't they just go?

The two looked at each other and the starch seemed to go out of them. Mrs. Albright met her gaze. "We came to apologize to you, Courtney."

"What?" The defensiveness wavered. It was hard to maintain defenses when the breath was knocked out of you.

"We misjudged you," Mr. Albright said.

"Our son did not grow into the man we'd have preferred him to be," his wife interjected diplomatically. "He tried numerous times and various schemes to extract money from us. Sadly, it worked most of the time. Not that we were stupid. We simply held out hope that he would change."

"He never did," the older man said. "The time came when we were forced to cut him off."

Not unlike what David's father had done, she thought. But in his case, the strategy was an unqualified success. Not for Joe.

"What do they call that these days? Tough love," the older man answered his own question.

"Tough on whom?" his wife said wryly. "I think it hurt us more than him. Especially in the long run."

"I don't understand." Courtney sat in the secondhand chair across from them.

Joe's mother twisted her fingers together in her lap. "We assumed that when our son came to us with the story of you being pregnant that it was another ploy for money. We had doubts that there was a baby. Even after she was born, we weren't convinced that—"

"She was Joe's?"

"Yes. And then we heard you'd named her Jane." Her eyes closed for a moment as she sighed. "We hardened ourselves to the probability that any young woman who would associate with our son was unsavory and disreputable."

"Ten-dollar words for *sleazy tramp*," Courtney commented.

Mrs. Albright winced. "We're not trying to hurt you, Courtney. Quite the contrary. We were wrong about you."

"James tried to make us see," her husband added.

"David's father?"

"Yes." The older man leaned back. "He'd gotten to know you, taken a liking to you, got you a job in the gift shop. Watched Janie grow up," he said wistfully.

"He was a good man." Courtney's chest felt tight. "I think about him a lot."

"As do we." Mrs. Albright said the words and her husband nodded sadly. "David is very much like his father," she added.

"Yes." A good man. The knot in Courtney's chest pulled a little tighter.

"He forced us to face the truth." Mrs. Albright met her gaze. "That Janie *is* our granddaughter. If you can forgive us, we would very much like the opportunity to get to know her."

"I—"

Just then the phone rang and Courtney was grateful for the distraction. She walked to the kitchen counter and answered it, hearing the crackle of a cell phone. "Hello?"

"Hi, Court. It's Susan Kier. I'm parked out front and I'm watching Janie walk to the door. She's on her way up."

"Thanks, Susan. I appreciate it."

"I'll see you tomorrow at the hospital."

"Sounds good. Next time it's my turn to keep the girls."

"You're on. Bye."

"Bye."

She looked back at the older couple. Minutes ago she'd wanted them gone before Janie got home. Now…

"Janie's on her way up. Excuse me a moment. I'm going to watch for her in the hall."

She walked out, leaving the door open, and listened to the sound of her daughter's steps on the stairs. When she appeared at the bottom of the last flight, Courtney smiled. "Hi, sweetie."

"Hi, Mommy. Mel and I baked cookies."

"All by yourself?"

"Her mom wouldn't let us. But we got to stir in chocolate chips and mix up the dough. And put it on the baking sheet."

"Did you eat any?"

"Yes. They were really good." Janie climbed the last stair and opened her arms for a hug.

"I'm glad you had a good time." Courtney gathered her closer than usual. She took a deep breath and said, "There's someone here to see you."

"There is?" Janie looked first excited, then confused. "Who?"

They walked inside and Janie stepped a little closer to Courtney's side when she spotted the older couple. "Janie, this is Mr. and Mrs. Albright."

"They have the same last name as me." She glanced up questioningly.

"They're your daddy's mother and father."

"They are?" Janie looked back at the sofa, her one visible eye wide.

"I see what David meant." Elizabeth Albright studied the little girl before she stood and moved in front of them.

"Do you know Dr. David?"

"I do indeed." She crouched down to little-girl level and at her age that couldn't be easy. That got her some positive points. "That's quite a boo-boo on your face."

"Dr. David's going to make me like I was before. Except for the dimple. But he said that will make me look mys— mystery— What's that word, Mommy?"

"Mysterious?" Courtney suggested.

"Yeah."

"Then I'm sure you'll be good as new," Mrs. Albright said. "But you're quite beautiful just as you are."

"That's what Dr. David told me, too."

The older woman stared in awe for several moments, then said, "This is your grandfather, and I'm your grandmother, Jane."

Janie looked up uncertainly, then back at the older woman. "It's nice to meet you."

"I'm very happy to meet you."

Janie glanced up doubtfully, then said, "Do you want to see my room?"

"I'd love to. But first I'd like to speak with your mother for a moment. Why don't you show your grandfather?"

"Okay." She walked over to the couch and said, "Want to see my room?"

"It would be my pleasure. But first I have to get up. I'm old," he said with a wink.

Courtney couldn't believe it. Crusty Morris Albright had winked at his granddaughter. Points to him for that. Next thing you knew lightning would strike.

Janie held out her small hand to him. "I could help you."

He took it and pretended to let her assist him to his feet. There was a suspicious thickness in his voice when he said, "Thank you. I needed that."

When they were alone, Courtney said, "I meant no disrespect in naming my little girl after—"

"—*my* little girl?"

"Yes. When I first met Joe, he talked about his sister. He seemed so caring and I fell hard and fast."

"Seemed caring?" The other woman nodded knowingly. "I suspect my son inflicted numerous emotional wounds and I appreciate the fact that you didn't rush to articulate them all."

"There's no reason to pile on," she said, remembering her complete humiliation and distress at learning Joe had really joined the military to run away from the responsibility of being a husband and father. There was no point in adding to his mother's grief. "And it serves no purpose to speak ill of the dead. Janie will only ever know that her father was a hero who died in the service of his country."

"That's very generous of you, Courtney."

"No. I'd do anything to protect my little girl."

"Then we have something in common," Mrs. Albright said. "Because I'd do anything to protect your little girl, too."

Emotion squeezed Courtney's throat as moisture filled her eyes. The surprise wasn't that Elizabeth Albright had made her cry, but the fact that she'd acknowledged Janie was family. "I appreciate that," she finally said.

Janie came running from the other room with Mr. Albright behind her. "Mommy, he—" She stopped and looked up. "What should I call you?"

"*Grandpa* has a nice ring to it," he said, looking at Courtney. She nodded and blinked rapidly.

"Then, by default, I'd be *Grandma*," Mrs. Albright said.

Janie frowned. "Whose fault?"

Everyone laughed.

"Never mind, sweetie."

"Can Grandma and Grandpa stay for dinner?" she asked.

"Of course. But are you hungry after all those cookies?"

Janie nodded enthusiastically. "Grandpa is going to play dolls with me."

"Are you sure?" she asked him.

"I've got a few years to make up for," he said, before being willingly dragged back down the hall.

"And I'd be pleased if you'd call me Elizabeth."

"It would be my pleasure," Courtney said sincerely.

The older woman drew in a shuddering breath before saying, "I'm glad you named her after Jane. It's fitting. That little girl is like a ray of sunshine from heaven. Thank you, Courtney for not throwing us out when you had every right to."

"How could I? You've given my child a gift. She has grandparents. How cool is that?"

"Very cool, indeed."

When Elizabeth leaned over and pulled her into a hug, Courtney felt every last trace of resentment slip away. David was right. The Albrights *were* good and decent people. And though Joe hadn't left Janie any money, he'd left her something money couldn't buy. A family.

Thanks to David, she was able to cash in on that. Courtney realized her debt to Dr. Hottie was mounting daily. And the days until he was gone were flying by.

As David climbed the three flights of stairs to Courtney's apartment, his respect and admiration for her soared while he pictured her lugging in groceries on a regular basis. If she and Janie weren't home, this cardiovascular workout would be for nothing. The target date for the little girl's surgery was fast approaching and he needed to check her out and see if there were any setbacks or contraindications to the procedure now.

He was here because of Janie, he told himself. And if he actually swallowed that line, there was probably beach-front property in Arizona someone would be more than happy to sell him.

On the landing in front of apartment 3, he blew out a long breath and let his heart rate return to normal. When he knocked and Courtney answered, the sight of her convinced him there was no such thing as a normal heart rate when he was near her.

"Hi," he said.

"Hi." There was surprise on her face. Also shadows in her eyes—and they were swollen and red.

Didn't take a rocket scientist to know she'd been crying. "What's wrong?"

"Would you believe nothing?"

"No." But he respected the fact she'd tried.

She blew out a long breath. "I got the insurance check today."

"That's good."

"Yeah. I can put a down payment on a skateboard."

"Court, can I—"

"I'm just feeling sorry for myself. The first of the month is looming and it seems like everything's due. I just worry." She shrugged. "And Janie's surgery is coming up. And I have to buy a car to replace the broken one. Don't mind me." She brushed the back of her hand over her cheek. "But you didn't stop by to hear me moan." She stared at him. "Why did you stop by?"

"House call. Take a look at Janie's face to see how the swelling looks."

Courtney leaned against the doorjamb. "That's very nice of you. But I'm sorry you came all this way, because she's not here at the moment."

He looked at his watch. It was after supper and time to be settling in for the evening, even if it was Friday night. "It's Friday night. Does she have a hot date?"

"Kind of."

"Oh?"

"Her grandparents stopped by yesterday."

"The Albrights?"

"Since there aren't any on my side of the family, those would be the ones." A small smile tugged at the corners of her lips. "You were right."

"Words to warm a man's heart. About what?"

"About them. They're very nice people. She's spending the night with them."

"Care to tell me how all this came about?"

It would sound as pathetic as it felt, but he wanted very much for her to invite him in. Another night alone at the Walnut River Inn was about as appealing as walking naked in a hail storm.

Courtney hesitated, and he held his breath. She was good at talking tough, but not so much at hiding her feelings. Conflict swirled in the depths of her huge brown eyes, churning up flecks of gold and green. Sensuality radiated from her like sound waves and need rolled through him as relentlessly as a line of thunderstorms pushing through tornado alley. Tucking a strand of hair behind her ear and chewing on her lip made her probably the sexiest thing he'd ever seen.

He'd dated models, actresses and TV personalities—all beautiful women. But there was so much more to Courtney than her looks. She had substance and a spine of steel. She was creative and loving and fiercely protective. And he'd never wanted anything more than an invitation to spend some time with her.

Finally, she stepped back and opened the door wider. "Come in. Would you like some coffee?"

"I don't want you to go to any trouble."

Her look was wry as she filled the coffeemaker with grounds and water, then flipped the on switch. "It would be easier to list the things I don't need to thank you for. Janie is over the moon about having a grandma and grandpa. They stopped by because of you. Because of whatever you said to them."

A few minutes later the coffee was made, and she poured two mugs that he carried into the living room. She sat on the sofa and David sat down beside her. When she angled her body sideways and tucked a foot beneath her, her knee grazed his thigh and set off sparks like a falling log on a campfire. He'd really wanted to see Janie, but he was far happier than he should be that he was alone with her mom.

"Thanks for the coffee."

She took the mug he held out. "It's the least I can do to show my appreciation."

"For what?"

He blew on his own. "I didn't do anything but give the Albrights something to think about."

"They apologized for misjudging me and admitted that in their eyes I was guilty by association with Joe. They're painfully aware that he had flaws and believed any woman who was with him had the same flaws."

"I see. What did you say?"

"That Janie would only know that her father was a hero." Her eyes were bleak when they locked with his. "I hate lying to her. Isn't a lie to protect her better than the awful truth?"

"For sure when she's little. I guess that's something you'll have to decide on a case-by-case basis as she gets older."

She took a sip of her coffee, then set it beside his on the table in front of them. "You mean if she's in danger of making the same mistake I did, I can hold myself up as a horrible warning."

"That's not exactly what I said."

"It's true, though." She wrapped her arms around her waist. "He definitely wasn't the poster boy for self-sacrifice. When I got pregnant, I thought he loved me because he insisted we get married. The truth is that he wanted to use me and his child to get money out of his parents."

Anger hummed through David and he struggled to remain expressionless. This was Courtney's story to tell and get off her chest. She didn't need his emotions getting in the way.

"At that point they were on to him," he pointed out.

"Yeah." She smiled without humor. "As hard as that was on me, I'm glad they didn't let him use them. Instead he used Uncle Sam."

"How so?"

"He didn't finish college and without skills he couldn't make a living. So he decided to join the army and see the world."

"The armed forces expect something out of their recruits."

"True. And he performed as needed. Putting on an act was as easy for him as breathing. Basic training and various assignments gave him an excuse to be away from me. The old ball and chain."

"Courtney, I'm sure—"

She held up a hand. "Don't say it. He never cared for me or his daughter. I'm not really sure why he didn't file for divorce, except that maybe he held out hope that his parents would come to their senses and cough up something for their granddaughter. He joined the army because he didn't want marriage or responsibility. He wanted to do what he wanted to do. He wanted freedom and women, and being stationed all over the country gave him exactly that—being away from me."

Joe Albright was a cold-hearted son of a bitch, David thought. He got lucky and found Courtney, had a beautiful little girl and walked away from it for the illusion of freedom. What really burned him up was that everyone believed the man a hero when he was nothing but selfish and self-centered.

"For what it's worth," he said, "I think this is one time when perpetuating the lie is the right thing."

"I'm not taking the easy way out for me," she protested. "I don't care for myself. It's hard on Janie. She doesn't understand why she never knew her father—" A sob choked off her words.

Courtney's tear-filled gaze met his own as moisture gathered in her eyes, then spilled over and trickled down her cheeks. "Oh, God. I'm sorry."

She scooted forward and started to stand. He put his hand on her arm. "Don't be sorry. There's no reason to apologize."

"The last thing you need is a weepy female. It's just—" The tears kept coming. "I didn't mean to say anything. It's just that I—I've been holding it in for so long."

She angled her body away and put her hands over her face. Instinct to comfort made David slide a forearm beneath her knees and one behind her back, then lift her into his lap and fold her in his arms. Curling against him, she shook with the weeping, deep wrenching sobs tore up from inside her. All he could do was hold her and be angry that she'd been used so badly. He tightened his arms around her because it was either that or put his fist through the wall. He wanted to hurt the man who'd hurt her, but doing damage to a ghost wasn't possible.

Finally, the emotional storm weakened and she sniffled. "I messed up your sweater."

"It'll dry," he said.

"I'll have it cleaned." She pulled back and the barest trace of humor sparkled in her red, swollen eyes. "Snot doesn't dry without leaving marks."

He laughed. "If it will make you feel better."

"It will. That and—" She ran a finger over his chest. "Thanks for—listening."

"My pleasure."

Her gaze locked with his and something electric arced between them. Something that said she wasn't vulnerable now.

David's body tightened with need, but he had a feeling this was more than just the physical release they could find in each other. He'd lived with a faint, hollow feeling in his gut for a very long time. It only went away when he was with Courtney. He wasn't about to make any promises based on this, but he knew for sure he'd regret it forever if he didn't kiss the living daylights out of her in the next second.

David touched his mouth to hers and sighed with satisfaction. Then she slid her hands over his chest and locked them around his neck, pressing herself fully against him as she nibbled small kisses over his lips. The banked fire inside him burst into flame and his heart went from zero to off the charts in three seconds flat. At this moment he couldn't care about right or wrong, and especially not the future.

There was only him, her and now.

Chapter Twelve

The second Courtney knew David intended to kiss her, every vow, every lecture, every warning she'd given herself about resisting him melted away. The why was a mystery to her, but this man—this sexy, handsome, successful, caring man—wanted her. Loneliness fell away and that felt so darn good. How was she supposed to stand firm against that?

Easy. She couldn't.

David took charge and settled his lips on hers, sending a delicious ache straight down the center of her body. He gently rubbed his hands down her back, over her arms even as he kept kissing her, demanding, making her want to give more. When he slid his warm palm beneath her sweatshirt and settled it on her bare skin, her breath caught.

He stopped and said against her mouth, "Is my hand cold?"

"Hardly. It's perfect. The healing touch."

"It's not healing that's on my mind."

"Or mine," she agreed.

He tucked her hair behind her ear, then rubbed a strand between two fingers. "Your hair is like silk."

The compliment produced a fast and furious jolt of pure lust. "Glad you like it."

"And your eyes." He stared directly into them. "Big, brown eyes. Warm. Soft."

She blinked at him. "Thank you, kind sir."

He grinned, then kissed the tip of her nose. "Cute. Saucy." He nipped her chin. "Stubborn."

"Flattery like that will turn my head," she said breathlessly.

After taking her earlobe gently in his teeth and nipping, he trailed his tongue down her neck, then blew softly on the wet skin in that oh-so-sensitive place. Her pulse instantly spiked and blood pounded in her ears.

And she desperately wanted to return the favor. She settled herself in his lap, straddling him, her legs on either side of his thighs. Resting her cast on his shoulder for balance, she traced a finger down one side of his neck while she nibbled kisses on the other side. His sharp intake of breath, along with little involuntary jumps of his muscles whenever she touched him, made her smile. It was incredibly arousing and she needed to feel her hands on his skin.

Leaning back, she took the bottom of his sweater and tugged up. He lifted his arms, eager to cooperate, and she pulled it off, tossed it aside. Then she went to work on the buttons of his long-sleeved white shirt. One by one she undid them, feeling her anticipation build as she watched the smoky look in his eyes simmer into a slow burn. She finished and pulled the shirt from the waistband of his jeans, then spread it wide and flattened her palm against his chest. His breathing grew more unsteady.

"You're playing with fire," he said, his voice husky with banked passion.

"It's been a long winter. I'm tired of being cold."

"I know just how to warm you up."

Without further warning, he pulled her sweatshirt up and over her head. After gently easing it off her left arm, he tossed it on top of his sweater. Then he traced a finger over her nipple, through her bra, and put a hitch in her breathing. She was definitely not cold any more. He reached behind her and expertly unfastened the hooks, then swept aside the flimsy material.

He cupped her breasts in his hands and brushed his thumbs over her nipples until they grew taut.

Dragging his gaze up to hers, he said in a ragged voice, "You are so beautiful."

Coming from him, the man who fixed the flaws nature dished out, that was high praise and it went straight to her head, nicking her heart on the way.

She kissed him slowly, softly, and sucked on his bottom lip before drawing back. "How odd that the less clothes I'm wearing, the hotter I get."

He braced his forearms under her butt and stood with her in his arms. "Then I think I know how to really warm you up."

Courtney knew where he was taking her, and she was all for it. But when he got to the doorway of her bedroom, she stopped him.

"What?" he asked.

"I just thought you should know that my bedroom is a virgin."

His eyes darkened. "Are you saying what I think you are?"

"I haven't been with anyone else in this room."

As the significance of her words sank in, he smiled. "But no pressure."

"Of course not."

"So the last time, when we were together in my room was—"

"My first time in a very long time."

"Duly noted," he said. "And appreciated. Are you trying to tell me you've changed your mind?"

"No. I just— I guess I just wanted you to know I don't make this a habit." She'd told him same thing last time, but it mattered very much that he believed her.

"It never occurred to me you did." He smiled. "So, are you ready to deflower the room?"

Wrapping her arms around his neck, she said, "Oh, yeah."

Chest to chest, skin to skin, he carried her to the bed then let her legs slide along his thighs until her feet touched the floor. He reached down and turned on the bedside lamp, the fringe of crystals around the shade catching the light.

Looking around he said, "*Deflower* is definitely the right word."

Seeing it through his eyes, she realized it was all girl. Floral comforter, curtains and throw pillows. Shades of pink, burgundy and olive green were everywhere.

"It works for me."

When the loneliness pressed relentlessly in on her, she comforted herself with the fact that there was no man she had to compromise for. No one to please but herself. Now with David, she wanted to compromise. Wanted to please.

She pulled down the quilt and blankets beneath, baring the sheets. When he reached out and flicked the button on her jeans, her stomach quivered. Then he lowered the zipper, his knuckles grazing her bare flesh and leaving sparks in their wake. Resting his big, gentle hands on her hips, he brushed her jeans and panties down her legs until she stepped out of them.

"Turnabout is fair play," she said.

She locked her gaze on his as she started to unbuckle his belt. Because she was clumsy with the cast on her left arm, he took over and finished, standing before her all muscle and flesh and masculinity. She ran her palm over the dusting of hair on his chest and savored the tingle of her skin. Being horizontal with David beside her seemed suddenly urgent. She sat on the bed and took his hand, sliding to the middle to make room for him. A heartbeat later the mattress dipped beneath his weight.

The chill of the cold sheets was chased away when he took her in his arms and pulled her to the hard, hot length of his body. He captured her mouth with his own and drew her top lip gently between his teeth. Then she felt his hand slide over her belly and lower, until he slipped a finger into her moist warmth. Sudden demand cut to her core and her breathing grew shallow and rapid. Something frantic built inside her and scratched to be liberated.

Reaching between them she took him in her hand, reveling in the hard and smooth contradictions of his texture. He sucked in a breath at her touch and tensed, his hands becoming eager as he stroked and molded. She felt the wild beat of his heart against her own and gloried in the feeling of power that she could wield.

He rolled her onto her back, then straddled her, pressing himself between her legs. Then, with one powerful thrust, he was inside her. He lifted her hips to go deeper and plunged. Her senses were filled with his taste and scent even as her body was filled with his essence. She felt the tension inside her build to breaking, just before her mindless cry of release ravished the virgin room.

David was only seconds behind her. He tensed just before shudders wracked his body. When it was over, he pressed his forehead to hers while their breathing returned to normal. Then he rolled onto his back and folded her into the shelter of his warm body.

"The room is happy and so is its occupant," she said, resting her hand on his chest and the hammering heartbeat that was still slowing.

"I'm glad."

"How did you know I needed you tonight?"

There was an almost imperceptible jump in his skin and he covered it well. She probably only noticed because she was so relaxed and suddenly he wasn't.

"Like you said—I'm the babe whisperer." His voice was casual but had a slight edge.

"Does that mean you think I'm a babe?"

"Unquestionably." But the fingers cupping her shoulder curled into a fist.

The body language was classic distance and she'd experienced it often enough with her husband to recognize the signs now. And just like that he booted her contentment out the door.

Surprisingly, David spent the night with her. When he'd grown detached last night, she'd thought he would stay in her bed long enough so it wouldn't look bad, then make some excuse and go. Instead, they'd fallen asleep in each other's arms and awakened in the same bed, as comfortable as if it happened every day.

She'd made breakfast, nothing fancy, just eggs and toast. He'd said it was the best he'd eaten in a long time, which was a bald-faced lie because she knew for a fact that Greta Stanford's breakfasts at the Walnut River Inn were to die for. Still, his compliment made her feel good. Happy. She hated happy because it didn't last and you somehow felt worse when it was gone.

So Courtney tried to get rid of him by mentioning that with Janie occupied at her grandparents, she was going to take the opportunity to look at cars. After he'd caught her in a cry the day before, she thought that would scare him off, but not so much. He'd insisted on coming along.

So here they were, walking around the lot at Reliable Used Cars on a beautiful March morning. It was on Lexington, just down the street from Buns 'n' Burgers. The temperature was a little chilly, but overhead the sky was a cloudless blue. With David beside her, happiness threatened to bubble to the surface and that made her nervous.

"It's awfully nice of you to go car-shopping with me."

"No problem. I'm at loose ends today. I—"

"Hi, folks." The salesman was short, portly and bald. The black leather jacket, although stylish, made him look like a hit man for the Sopranos.

"Hi," Courtney said.

"My name is Chad. And you are?" He looked at David.

"I'm Courtney and this is David," she said.

"Nice to meet you," he answered shaking hands. "Something for the missus?" he asked, looking at David again.

"He's not my mister. I'm buying the car." A breeze kicked up and blew her hair across her face. She tucked it behind her ear. "I need something that's in good shape. Fuel economy is important," she added. "And the crash-test safety is a concern."

"And you want to spend a dollar and a half," Chad teased.

"Exactly."

"I'll show you some of my best deals. You pick something out and take it for a spin. Then we'll talk deal."

"Okay."

When she'd decided on a small compact, Chad led them into his office/cubicle, complete with cluttered metal desk, computer and two chairs. She and David sat. She told him what she intended to put down and he left to crunch numbers with the dealership's financial guy.

Courtney looked at David. "This is the part that makes me nervous."

"Did you like the car?"

"Yeah. It's in decent shape as far as I can tell. The gas mileage is good. Peppy for a compact. And it's red."

"Color is important?" His grin was teasing.

"Of course. I need wheels, but preferably without a body that's neon-green or puce."

He frowned. "What shade would that be?"

"Not a clue. I'd have to look it up in the dictionary," she admitted. "What do you think of it?"

"Pretty much the same. Although I'd prefer a zippy silver model. And it couldn't hurt to have it checked out by an independent mechanic." He thought for a second. "Also an extended warranty, if it's available, wouldn't be a bad idea."

"Both good thoughts, but not especially economical," she said. "My budget is screaming for mercy now, and that's without a car payment." She twisted her fingers together. "How long does it take to run a few numbers?"

"Maybe it won't be as bad as you think." David reached over and took her hand in his own.

"Maybe." But she'd learned in her life that not only was it always as bad as she thought, usually it was worse.

When Chad walked in and sat behind the desk looking supremely confident, Courtney knew it was the latter.

"I think you're going to like this payment," he started. He put a piece of paper in front of her with monetary amounts scattered over it. Then he circled one. "That's a steal."

Her stomach dropped, then knotted up. Tears that smacked of desperation were very close to the surface. "Thank you, Chad. I'll—" She was trying to think of a polite way to say "not in this lifetime."

David slid forward and glanced at the numbers. "It's not a bad price. I'd like to talk about throwing in that extended warranty."

"Are we talking about a done deal here?" Chad asked.

"Yes," David said.

"What?" Courtney stared at him. "David, I'm not sure I can handle the payment."

"You won't have to," he said.

Why wouldn't she have to? What was he saying? She looked at Chad. "Can you give us a minute?"

"Sure thing." He stood. "I'll check with my manager on that extended warranty."

"You do that." David met her gaze.

When they were alone, she slid forward on the chair and angled her knees toward him. "What do you mean I won't have to handle the payments?"

"Because the loan will be paid off."

"By who? My fairy godmother?"

"Be reasonable, Court."

"When did I start being unreasonable?"

"Look." David sat up straighter. "I want to help."

"Just so I get it right before I become unreasonable, I'd like to clarify something. By *help* you mean buy this car for me outright?"

"I can afford it."

"That's not what I asked. Do you or do you not intend to pay for this car?" When he started to answer, she said, "A simple yes or no will suffice."

"All right then. Yes."

"Why, David?"

"Because you need it."

"And I'll figure something out," she protested.

"What's to figure? I'll write a check." He shrugged. "The money isn't going to make a difference to me one way or the other. But you're raising a child and could use the help. It's as simple as that."

If something looked too good to be true, Courtney had learned that it usually was. No one in her world had ever done something without expecting a return on the investment. More than likely there was something in this for David.

"*Simple* is hardly the word I would use," she said.

"What does that mean?"

"I have to ask this. What do you get out of buying me a car?"

"The satisfaction of giving assistance to a hard-working single mom." His gaze narrowed.

"That's it?"

"What else could there be?" The irritation in his voice said there'd been a direct hit on a nerve.

"Oh, I don't know," she said. "Maybe it's about putting a muzzle on your conscience when you go back to L.A. with your hometown hero hat firmly in place."

"What the hell does that mean?" he said.

"It means we've had a good time. I'm not denying that. I like you, David. I appreciate what you've done, what you're going to do for Janie. Believe me, I know I sound like an ungrateful hag, but it's got to be about more than giving me a helping hand."

"Do you know how paranoid that sounds?"

"It's not paranoia if someone's out to get you," she shot back.

Chad walked back in and glanced warily between the two of them. "If you're paying cash, my manager authorized me to give you—"

"Hold that thought," Courtney said. She stood. "I'll have to get back to you on this."

"David?" Chad looked to him.

He stood and blew out a long breath. "We have to talk this over."

"I can't guarantee—"

"Good-bye, Chad." Courtney walked out and kept walking.

She would have walked all the way home if David hadn't taken her arm and steered her wordlessly to his BMW parked in the lot. Neither of them said a word on the way back to her apartment. In her case it was because she didn't trust herself not to cry and she'd done enough of that in front of David. When he pulled up in front and turned off the car, she opened the passenger door and started to get out.

"Court?"

She made the mistake of looking at him and when she did something in the region of her chest grew tight and achy. "What?"

"Can we talk about this?"

"What is there to say?"

"Aren't you being overly suspicious?" he asked, resting his wrist on the steering wheel.

It was such a blatantly masculine thing to do and oddly sexy. And the fact that she noticed at all when she was so angry and upset really ticked her off.

"If I'm exceptionally suspicious, it's not without good reason." Still in the seat, she pulled the door closed against the wind and stared out the front window. She didn't trust herself to look at him. "My father lost himself in a bottle of whiskey and left me to raise myself and take care of him. He was never there for me. I thought Joe was different, but I was wrong. He just left me in a different way, because he was never there to begin with. He ran out on me and looked like a hero when he did. I learned the hard way that I can only ever count on myself." She looked at him. "I can't accept the kind of help you're offering and I don't understand why you're doing it."

"I truly do want to help. Not because of some imagined payoff, a way to not feel guilty for going back to my practice." He blew out a long breath. "Although there's probably some truth to the guilt part, but it's not what you think."

"Then what is it?" she asked.

"When I told you about the falling out with my father, I left out the details."

She closed her eyes and stifled a groan. This was where she felt like the world's biggest jerk. If only she hadn't looked at him, she'd be safely inside. She was going to hate herself for asking, but that couldn't be helped. "What details?"

"I fell in love. At least I thought I did, and all I could think about was being together forever. But she was flunking a class and I was prepared to do whatever I could to make sure she didn't get kicked out of school."

"If the story had a happy ending there would have been no disagreement with your father."

"You're right about that." Grimly, he shook his head. "On the final exam I was going to slip her the answers, but I got caught."

"Oh, David—"

"I finally got my father's attention." He laughed, but the sound was bitter and dark. "To make a long story short, he said he didn't raise me to be a cheat. Stupidly I said he didn't raise me at all because he was never there, so who was really the family disgrace? He couldn't condone or support cheating or anyone who engaged in such reprehensible behavior. I was on my own in every way, including financial."

She didn't know what to say so she asked, "What happened with the girl?"

His expression was wry but his eyes darkened with anger and bitterness. "She let me take the fall, then dumped me."

She sucked in a breath at the callousness. She knew what young love felt like. She knew what being used felt like. It made you not want to put your heart on the line again. And David lost his father, too. And his support. Yet he'd found a way to go on. How had he managed it? "You've told me that you still became a doctor. I guess what I'd like to know is…how?"

"With the black mark on my record, I couldn't transfer any credits, so I had to start over. Fortunately the lesson came early in my academic career. I got student loans, grants, scholarships and worked my ass off because school was all I had."

Because he'd lost the father he'd spent his whole life trying to impress. It all made sense now. The charity work. Helping Janie and her. David's core belief was that if he did enough good it would cancel out that one bad decision and make things right. The problem was that all the good deeds in the world wouldn't give him the absolution he craved from the father who was gone forever and couldn't give it to him.

"I'm so sorry, David."

"Not your fault." He shrugged. "The story is as old as Adam, Eve and the apple. Boy meets girl. Boy falls head over heels and when girl bats her eyelashes and says she needs him, boy wants to fix problem."

Needs. That word was like a punch to the gut.

Courtney remembered how he'd reacted after making love, when she'd said she'd needed him. He'd grown distant and his behavior today was all about pushing her buttons in the worst possible way—because he knew she wanted to be independent. Correction, because she had told him more than once that she could take care of herself.

"So—" She swallowed. "When I said I needed you last night— It was a red flag for you."

He glanced sharply at her. "What are you talking about?"

"You…withdrew, I guess is the best way to say it."

"No—"

"I know what it feels like when a man pulls away from me, David. The thing is, I'm not asking for anything."

"I never said you were." His voice was deep, dangerous.

"That defensive tone says you're not being honest with yourself. We shared something pretty wonderful. And, for that moment, I needed you. I'm healing physically and emotionally. It wasn't about forever."

He smiled, but it was his bedside manner face. The one he hid behind because he'd been used and thrown away and lost everything. "Okay."

But she knew it wasn't okay and never would be. He had no reason to trust that she wouldn't take his heart and throw it away. And she didn't trust him to be there for her.

"I guess we have something in common."

"What's that?" he asked.

"Neither of us wants to be used."

He frowned. "I'm not using you."

"Yes, you are. I'm the latest in a long list of charity cases. If you help enough people, you'll get back what you lost with your father."

His gaze narrowed as his eyes darkened. "You should give up the business major and take up Psych 101."

"It doesn't require an advanced degree to understand you. The dots were all there and you just connected them." She took a deep breath and opened the car door, then stepped out. She leaned down and looked at him. "Like I said before, you've got demons, David. And so do I. But the bottom line for me is that Janie and I will not be your current pity project."

"That's not—"

"Good-bye, David." She closed the door and it took all her self-control not to look back as she went to the door of her building and let herself inside. When she was out of sight, she rested her forehead against the cool wall.

What ticked her off the most was that she couldn't even blame him for how much she hurt. She knew what it was like to have nothing and David did too. She understood why he was protecting himself. Why should he believe that she wasn't after him for what he could give her? He had no reason to believe that her refusing his generosity wasn't simply a ploy to manipulate him before reeling him in.

He would never let down his guard to care about her. He had no reservations about making her his pity project, but the real pity was that she'd fallen in love with him.

Chapter Thirteen

It was the pity-project crack that finally pushed David to make the call.

During the last two days, the whole conversation with Courtney had gotten him to thinking about his father. If he was being honest with himself, he'd been remembering James Wilder since learning he'd died and there wouldn't ever be a chance to make things right between them.

David had never told anyone about what happened. There was no way to put into words the depth of disgust, disappointment and disgrace he'd seen in his dad's eyes. That look had carved out an empty feeling inside him and nothing he'd done since had come close to filling it up.

Then he got to thinking about why he'd done what he'd done, pushed the envelope the way he had. He'd had a lot of time to think, what with not being able to sleep. A lot of motivation for his behavior went back to his childhood, when his father had brought Anna home. Then his parents had adopted her and said, *She's your sister now.* Translation: *You have to love her.* From an adult perspective, it was like a man bringing home his secretary and telling his wife to love and accept the interloper.

David realized that a lot of the resentment he felt toward his father was entrenched in memories of the attention lavished on Anna. His parents took her in as an infant when she'd been abandoned. His feelings were childish and stupid, and he was an idiot times ten, but that didn't alter the fact that it was past time to deal with it.

He realized he knew very little about Anna's life since he'd left home. Opening his laptop on the desk in his room he accessed the wireless Internet connection and signed on. Courtney had used it to find out about him. He typed in *Anna Wilder.* What he found only amplified his negative feelings.

She was working for the company trying to take over the hospital.

He called and after being transferred several times, was put through to her secretary.

"Anna Wilder's office. How may I help you?"

"I'd like to speak with Ms. Wilder."

"May I tell her who's calling?"

"Tell her it's Dr. David Wilder."

"Hold, please."

He held just long enough to consider the possibility that she was going to blow him off. Then he heard a click and a woman's voice.

"Hello, David." The voice was coolly polite. "How did you get this number?"

"I looked you up on the Internet."

"Ah."

"It's a sad commentary on our family that we have to use the Web to find out what's going on with each other." Hypocritical, he knew. But he was in kind of a black mood and figured the pot calling the kettle black sort of went with the territory.

Anna ignored the dig. "How are you?"

"Fine. And you?" He stood and paced the room.

"Couldn't be better." There was an awkward silence before she said, "To what do I owe the pleasure of a phone call from the famous physician to the stars?"

"I've been doing a lot of thinking since Dad's funeral."

"Me, too." There was a deep sigh. "Something like that— Losing him—"

He couldn't be sure, what with the cell phone connection, but it almost sounded like she choked up. "Yeah. I know. It makes you take stock of your life."

"Yeah," she agreed. "It does. And in that spirit, how is your life?"

"Busy." But empty. And the feeling had gotten worse, lonelier somehow, after the way Courtney had called him on his behavior yesterday. "And like Ella and Peter I'm guessing by that physician-to-the-stars crack you're under the impression that all I do is implants and nose jobs."

"No?"

The teasing note in her voice brought back memories of her when they were growing up. Her light blond hair and blue eyes. All the intensity in her waiflike, Precious-Moments-doll expression. She would argue her opinion first, then ask questions later. Always on the defensive.

"No," he said. "As a matter of fact, I've taken trips to developing countries and done facial reconstruction on kids with some pretty severe injuries."

"Doctors without Borders?"

"No. But a similar organization." Why did he feel the need to tell her and not Peter or Ella? Didn't take a shrink to point out that neither of his siblings made him feel the need to be special enough to earn his father's affection.

"That's great, David. It must be very rewarding. So is there anyone special in your life? Are you dating someone?"

Courtney's face flashed into his mind along with the reminder that she believed he was using her to cancel out his youthful indiscretion. It was impossible for her to let herself believe that some good deeds don't have an ulterior motive. Whether or not she trusted his reasons, he was going to fix Janie's face. Then he'd return to his practice. Move forward.

Alone.

The thought was like being swallowed by a big, black hole. It was as if all the light and color were suddenly sucked out of his world. His chest felt like someone had whacked him a good one to shock his heart into normal sinus rhythm. When he left Courtney would his heart stop for good?

"Earth to David?"

"Hmm?"

"Thought I lost you for a second. The question wasn't that hard. Are you dating anyone special?"

Courtney was special, but they weren't exactly dating. And after yesterday he was pretty sure she didn't like him very much. "No. How about you?"

"How about me—what?"

"Is there a man in your life?"

"No. My job is pretty demanding—" She stopped. Probably because of the can of worms she'd opened.

He took the ball and ran with it. "What the hell are you doing working for Northeastern HealthCare? The last I heard you were in Mergers and Acquisitions at a large Manhattan investment bank. Peter and Ella have no idea you're working to undermine them."

"I saw a lot of potential for growth with this company. And I'm not hiding anything. You found me."

"Growth? You call growth swallowing up everything in your path?"

"Size matters, David. If it didn't, all those Hollywood starlets wouldn't flock to your office so you could give them bigger breasts."

"It's all part of the service. They're going to do it anyway. At least I can do the job right and make sure there are no medical complications that will compromise their health down the road."

"And you put a silencer on your conscience by fixing kids?"

It they'd been face to face, she'd have seen him flinch at that zinger. "It's not about me—"

"And my job isn't about me. It's for the greater good. Bigger means revenue that can be channeled into research, equipment, programs to actually help people."

"Walnut River General Hospital *is* helping people. If it ain't broke, don't fix it."

"What's wrong with making it better?" she argued.

"You should stop buying the company policy hook, line and sinker, Anna. Northeastern HealthCare isn't known for improving the facilities they acquire. They have more of a scorched-earth policy. Suck the life out of it and move on."

"Some things never change," she said, her voice cool again.

"What does that mean?"

"I mean putting down my job."

"This isn't about you, Anna." Staring out the window, he thought about that and shook his head. "Maybe partly. How can you live with yourself? Is career advancement worth betraying your father?"

"I'm good at what I do. Dad would have been proud of me," she said defensively.

"Proud that you're helping destroy his work?" He gentled his voice. If anyone understood the yearning for a father's pride and respect, it was him. But he couldn't let this go unchallenged. "Dad and Mom took you in, gave you a home, made you part of the family. They loved you. Now you're repaying that by undermining the institution he gave his life for."

"David," she said with exaggerated patience. "We're coming at this from two different directions—business and medicine."

"That's because they're diametrically opposed."

"It doesn't have to be that way. You have the skill to heal people, but you're also a businessman. You have office space, staff, supplies and it doesn't come cheap. There's a common ground where business and health care can co-exist—"

"Don't patronize me, Anna. If this was good for the hospital, Peter would be on board. He's a pretty smart guy and he's opposed to this takeover. It's not in the hospital's best interest and I'm guessing deep down inside you know it, too."

"Oh, please—"

"Why is it that no one in the family knows you work for Northeastern HealthCare?"

"How do you know they don't?" she asked.

"Because I'm pretty sure Peter would have mentioned it when he told me what's going on. If you were a doctor, you'd understand what this is going to do to the people in town."

There was a long silence before she said in icy tones, "It's clear that we have to agree to disagree."

"Look, Anna, I didn't call to argue with you. I really wanted to—"

"I'm sorry, David. I've got another call I have to take."

"Wait, Anna—"

"Good-bye, David."

There was a click on the other end and he sighed as he flipped his cell closed. That went well, he thought. Not. Whatever he'd been looking for, he hadn't achieved the goal. But he got the feeling that he and Anna did have one thing in common—the need for their father's approval. It was a terrible thing to disappoint a parent. He wasn't sure why his sister felt that way, but his own sins stood out in stark relief against the blackness of his soul.

Despite what Courtney had said, he wasn't using her or Janie to ease his conscience. He genuinely cared about them. From the first moment he'd seen them, battered and bruised, but not bowed, the Albright women had taken hold of his heart and wouldn't let go.

As he looked out the window at the grass, trees and bushes just starting to show signs of spring, the thought of caring about a woman that way made his blood run cold. He'd learned that tender emotion was like an explosive device that could detonate without warning. The repercussions were painful and life-altering.

Trying not to let on that she was apprehensive, Courtney held Janie's hand as they walked into the medical exam room. It was a suite for visiting doctors to see patients, located in the tower behind the main building of Walnut River General Hospital. David had left a message on her cell asking them to meet him here so he could take a look at Janie's face and determine whether or not to schedule the reconstruction. The nurse was Susan Kier, the mother of Janie's best friend. A familiar face was comforting since the two of them were pretty jumpy.

Courtney looked around. It was a typical room with the exam table, sink and anatomy posters sharing space with various drug advertisements on the beige walls.

"Okay, J.J., if you'll just hop up there on the exam table." Susan Kier slid the foot stool over so Janie could climb up. She was the only one who shortened Jane Josephine to J.J. Janie liked it.

"Thanks, Mrs. Kier." The paper covering the table crackled when the little girl sat and settled.

When all was quiet, Courtney said, "I didn't know you worked here in the tower."

"I don't." Susan took the blood-pressure cuff from the wall and secured it around the small arm while Janie watched in fascination as she squeezed the black bulb and pumped it up. "At least not full-time. But when there's a guest doctor here, the nurses take turns assisting when he, or she, is seeing outpatients."

"That was tight on my arm," Janie said.

"Sorry, J.J. It has to be snug to get a good reading. But it's all done now." After making a notation in the chart, Susan looked up. "James Wilder believed patients' health issues resolved faster with a personal touch. He'd be pleased that the hospital is continuing in the spirit and standard of care he championed while he was with us. He'd be enormously proud of both of his sons."

"Yes, he would," Courtney said.

She knew the man who was the closest thing to a father she'd ever known would have fought the takeover by Northeastern HealthCare just as hard as his son Peter. And whether David wanted to admit it or not, he was his father's son, too.

It had been a week since their disastrous excursion to the used-car lot. A thousand times since she'd wished to call back the words. They were abrasive, ungrateful and he didn't deserve the abuse. A simple "no, thank you" would have been sufficient. But she had to go psycho-babble on him. The ugly, selfish truth was that she'd instinctively pushed him away to protect herself. The problem was, it was like closing the barn door after the cows got loose, because she'd already fallen in love with him.

Susan smiled at them. "Okay, you two, I'll be just outside if you need anything. Dr. Wilder should be here in a few minutes."

"Thanks, Susan."

"Bye, Mrs. Kier."

"When you're finished with the doctor, J.J., how about I take you to the cafeteria for ice cream?"

"Can I, Mom?" Even with only one eye showing—especially with one eye showing—Janie's face took on a pleading, puppy-dog expression that worked big-time.

Courtney sighed. "How can I say no?"

"Then we've got a date." Susan closed the door softly.

Courtney stared after her and realized it was easier not to be scared when she didn't have to be the strong one all by herself. Janie was relying on her for reassurance and when puppy-dog changed to worried, anxious and nervous, she forced herself to smile cheerfully even though breaking down in tears held a lot more appeal.

"That's nice of Mrs. Kier to take you for ice cream," she said, trying to distract her daughter.

"Is it going to hurt, Mommy?"

"What? When Dr. David looks at your face?" When Janie nodded uncertainly, she shook her head. "He's just going to see if the swelling has gone down enough so that he can fix it."

"Is it going to hurt when he fixes it?"

Courtney winced inwardly. It was an invasive procedure and there was no way to do it without discomfort. She didn't believe in lying, but it was important to choose her words carefully.

"Well, sweetie, it's unlikely that—"

The door opened suddenly and she was incredibly happy to see David. For so many reasons. But relief at not having to answer was at the top of the list. Also very high up was the fact that he made the white lab coat look sexy.

"Hi," she said brightly.

"Dr. David!" Janie held out her arms and he walked over to give her a hug.

"Hi, you two." He stepped back and stuck his hands in the pockets of the lab coat. "How are you?"

"Okay," Janie said.

"Me, too," Courtney added. She noticed circles under his eyes and lines on either side of his nose and mouth. For a man taking a rest from work, he looked not very rested. She stood on one side of Janie and he was on the other. "Have you been sleeping? You look tired."

"I'm fine." He turned his attention to his patient. "Let's see how this looks, princess."

"I'm not a princess."

"Says who?" With the long fingers of one hand, he held her small chin still while he carefully removed the tape and gauze bandages.

"Says Mommy." Holding very still, Janie slid her a look from the corner of her good eye. "She says I'm not a princess. Just a regular girl."

Courtney wasn't looking straight on but could still see the damage. Where Janie's cheekbone should have been, there was what she could only think of as a hollow, a depression. The dimple that matched the good side of her face was missing in action.

David glanced at her and somehow the expression in his eyes told her not to worry. Everything would be fine if she trusted him.

"I hate to be the one to tell your mommy she's wrong," he said, "but you're not a regular girl. You're special."

He tilted Janie's face up and gently touched the area around the trauma. "Does that hurt?"

"No."

"How about this?" he asked.

Janie shook her head.

"Good." He brushed her hair off her forehead and playfully tweaked her nose. "The swelling has receded nicely. I'd like to schedule the repair as soon as possible."

Courtney didn't know whether to laugh or cry. She wanted

this over and done with. Put behind them. A distant memory. At the same time she knew that when all of the above happened, she and David would be done with. A distant memory. But it would be best to take it one trauma at a time. She'd think about her own heart damage later because she'd reached the worry threshold and just couldn't hold any more.

"How do we arrange it?" she asked him.

"Susan will set it up with the hospital." Instead of calling the nurse, he replaced the bandage on the injured half of Janie's face.

When he finished, she said, "Dr. David?"

"What, princess?" He gave her his undivided attention.

She twisted her fingers in her lap. "Is it gonna hurt when you make it better?"

He met her gaze directly, without hesitation. "You know I won't lie to you."

Janie thought for a moment, then nodded. "Yes. Because you said you'd come to my school for awards night and you did."

"Okay. This is what's going to happen. Your mom is going to bring you to the hospital. We're going to give you some medicine so you'll go to sleep when I fix your face. You won't feel any pain. When you wake up, there will be some discomfort. But we can give you something to make it not so bad until it's gone for good. Do you believe that I'm going to make you better?"

Without hesitation, she said, "Yes."

He called Susan back in and asked her to set up a surgical date, then said, "When it's arranged, Susan will let you know and you'll be given pre-surgery instructions."

"Mommy? Can I go have ice cream now?"

"Of course. I'll meet you there after I talk with David."

David started to lift Janie from the exam table and she put her arms around his neck and hugged tightly. "I'm only a little scared now, Dr. David."

He pressed her close. "I'm going to take extra special care of you, princess."

When he set her down, she slipped her hand into Susan's and the two left. David turned back and frowned. "What's wrong, Court?"

Tears filled her eyes when she said, "I'm a lot scared."

Without hesitation, he pulled her into his arms. "I can't tell you not to be. It wouldn't do any good."

What did her good was being right where she was. She pressed her cheek against his solid chest and listened to the strong, steady beat of his heart and tried not to hate herself for relying on him. It wasn't as though she was going to make it a habit, but he was here now and she needed him.

"You're her mom and I think worrying about facial reconstruction is part of the job description," he said.

Moments ago it seemed impossible that she could laugh, but she did. "I can't argue with that."

"Wow." He rubbed his chin on the top of her head. "You not arguing. Let me mark the date on my calendar so I can remember it always."

"Smart aleck."

He tightened his hold. "I promise you that I will do my best. I'll take extraordinary care of your child."

"I know you will. You're extraordinarily wonderful with her."

"It's easy. She's a wonderful kid."

"Your father would be very proud of the man you are," she said, sliding her arms beneath the lab coat and around his waist. "In fact, of all of his children. Susan and I were just commenting on the fact that his memory and spirit are still alive in this hospital and the personal care offered."

He tensed, just before he dropped his hands and stepped back. His expression was grim. "That may not be enough to keep it going."

"What do you mean?" She touched his arm and ignored

the shiver of awareness that jolted her system like defibrillator paddles. "What's wrong, David?"

"I had a long talk with my sister, Anna."

"That's good, right? Communication and all that."

He shook his head. "Not when she's communicating that she works for the company trying to take over this hospital."

"You didn't know?"

"No. And I don't think Peter and Ella do either. I've got to break the news."

"Did you try to talk to her?" Courtney asked, shocked that a member of the Wilder family was in the enemy camp, so to speak.

"Of course I did. She grew up in the same house as the rest of us. She knows how much time and energy our father put into building the hospital. All the blood, sweat and tears that went into giving it a heart and soul. Molding the mission statement to put the care in patient care. My sister is a company person all the way and to her it's just a business."

"And?"

He shoved his hand through his hair. "She's essentially on the team that's destroying my father's dream. She's tearing down the life's work of the man who gave her a home and family."

"I'm sorry the conversation didn't go well." She took his hand and linked her fingers with his. "Maybe if you and Peter talk to her together—"

"I don't think so." He slid his hand from hers. "You don't understand. My father doted on her because she was an orphan. But adding Anna to the mix changed the family dynamic. My mother withdrew emotionally. I can't speak for Ella and Peter, but I resented being pushed aside. She took all the affection and attention and instead of thanking her lucky stars, she's siding with the enemy. Just goes to show what happens when you give up everything for a woman."

Courtney went cold inside as her heart interpreted the message. He would never get over the trauma of being used and abused by a woman. And there was no surgical procedure to repair the invasive trauma he'd experienced. She didn't know the rug was there until he'd pulled it out from under her.

"David," she said gently, struggling to keep her voice even. "Maybe I don't understand. My upbringing was about as dysfunctional as it gets. Your father was the first to show me what a caring, considerate man looks like. So I have no frame of reference for growing up in a family that gives a damn about you. But I'm pretty sure that your father would be deeply troubled if he knew that the message you took away from giving an abandoned child a home is not to love at all."

There was nothing left to say so she walked out, down the hall and around the corner. When he didn't come after her, she ducked into the ladies' room and struggled to breathe against the crushing pain inside her.

She'd finally met a man who was as selfless and noble as he appeared to be. A man who didn't have an ulterior motive. A man who made her want to give her love, which was all she had to give. But he was also a man who would never accept her love because that meant he had to risk caring again.

She felt as though she'd been fighting her whole life. To get ahead. To make something of herself. For survival. But there was no way to fight this. And the sadness of it went clear to her soul.

Chapter Fourteen

After checking the O.R. scheduling for Janie's surgery the following day, David brushed by someone as he headed toward the E.R. exit on his way out of the hospital.

"If it isn't the hotshot, golf-playing face-lifter from La La Land."

The mocking female voice was painfully familiar and David turned to see his sister Ella. She grinned and waggled her fingers at him. "I thought that might get your attention."

His little sister was paraphrasing what Courtney had said about him after their first meeting. After her earlier remark about disappointing his father, he figured Court would stand by her first impression.

"Hi, El." He smiled back, but his heart wasn't in it. "For the record, I don't play golf."

"Beach volleyball?" she teased.

"Hardly. To maintain this godlike physique, I have a treadmill, elliptical and weights from the sporting goods store. All tucked away in a spare bedroom."

"It's working," she said, giving him a once-over. "What are you doing here?"

"Making sure everything's set for Janie's surgery tomorrow."

"Excellent." She smiled. "I'm so glad I called you. And that you came, of course. Janie couldn't be in better hands. You're good, but you're also family. Courtney's worked here for so long, she's like family and families look out for each other."

"Yeah." That's the way it should be. Although you couldn't prove it by him.

"What's wrong, handsome?"

"Nothing. Don't be dramatic, El—"

She frowned at the bustling E.R., then tugged him into the quietest corner of the waiting room, beside a silk plant. "Don't play that game. I'm your sister, and I'm not blind. I know when something's on your mind, so spill it, David."

Her soft, pretty features tensed into determination and he knew there'd be no escape until he—shudder—talked. "You're not going to drop this, are you?"

"Not even for money. What's putting lines in that pretty face of yours?"

He snorted at her compliment, then turned serious. "It's something Courtney said."

Instantly his sister looked troubled. "I was teasing a minute ago. I'm sure she no longer thinks you're a shallow surgeon from L.A."

He shook his head. "That's ancient history, sis. She had some razor-sharp comments about my relationship—or lack thereof—with Dad."

"What did she say?"

"I'd rather not get into it."

"Bet you'd talk to Dad—if he was here." Sadness crept into her dark eyes.

"When I need to talk to him the most, he went and died on me. Damned inconvenient."

"Yeah, I'm sure he's not real tickled about it either," Ella said dryly.

"This isn't being shallow, El," he protested. "It's more about feeling sorry for myself."

"And you clarified that because self-pity is so much more attractive?"

"I didn't say that. It's the simple truth."

And it wasn't just because he'd lost his father, who could have been his best friend, and would never get back the wasted years. Somehow Courtney was all mixed up in these feelings, too. He didn't know how to fix it and that was damned frustrating for a man whose whole life was about fixing what was broken.

"Okay, then," Ella said. "As long as you're being honest about your pity party, I suggest you take it somewhere it will do some good."

He stared at her for a moment. "That bracing little piece of advice made absolutely no sense to me, El."

"Then let me put it bluntly. Go talk to Dad."

"You might want to have your head examined, and you've come to the right place, I might add." He touched two fingers to her forehead, teasingly checking to see if she was feverish. "Can you say CT scan?"

"I'm serious, David. I've had the same feeling about wanting to talk to him. So I go to the graveyard, to his headstone, and—" She shrugged sheepishly. "Talk."

"You're kidding, right?"

She shook her head and looked a little hurt. "It always makes me feel better. But go ahead and laugh. I heal broken bones for a living, what do I know about feelings?"

He knew he'd hurt hers. "I'm sorry. It's just a little far out."

"Dad's a little far out now, which is why it works. Besides, confession is good for the soul. The upside of baring that soul in the graveyard is that it's full of souls who don't talk back. At least we hope they don't." She nodded for emphasis. "Look, I've got to get back to work. Good luck with the surgery tomorrow."

"Thanks."

It wasn't the procedure that bothered him, but what would happen after. That was the part where he left town and the thought was about as appealing as—well, talking to a ghost.

If anyone saw him talking to himself in the cemetery there'd be no doubt he was crazy. But it was certainly a beautiful day for crazy, David thought. The sky was clear and blue, as it could only be in Walnut River. April was approaching and dragging spring along for the ride as the grass turned green and trees were beginning to bud. Bouquets of flowers and plants dotted the cemetery's rolling hills.

He parked the BMW in the sector where his father had been buried, then turned off the engine. Was this really insane? Or did it just feel that way?

After locking the car, he laughed. Who was going to steal the thing in a cemetery? Then he started walking and headed for his father's eternal resting place and the maple that shaded it. The tree was easy to find, the tallest one around. And how fitting was that? He'd always had the impression that James Wilder was the tallest, strongest, wisest person on the face of the earth. Now his father was under it and the emotion brought on by the thought made his throat and chest tight.

He coughed, then tentatively said, "Hi, Dad. Long time no see."

And he would never see him again. Looking around at the tree branches swaying and rustling in the breeze, he remembered the saying—if a tree falls in the forest and no one is there to hear, does it still make a sound? "Here's a philosophical question. If a man talks to his dead father and no one is there to hear, is he still crazy?"

No one answered. Good thing.

The simple headstone was in place, with the dates of his father's birth and death and the words, "Do no harm."

"The Hippocratic Oath," David whispered.

Every doctor swore first to do no harm in the treatment of patients. But sometimes an invasive procedure was required for the greater good. Like Janie, he thought. He had to go in to repair her shattered cheekbone. No pain, no gain.

"Dad, I know you never understood why I wanted to go into plastics. Ella is in orthopedics. Peter is following in your footsteps. And I'm the black sheep—Botox and boob jobs. Superficial stuff. It's not practicing medicine in your opinion. Once a screw-up, always a screw-up."

He let out a long breath as he ran his fingers through his hair. "You always said that a doctor uses every skill, all the science and a black bag full of tricks to cheat death. And no one questions that. But what about after that, Dad? What happens to the scars? What if they're so bad a person wants to hide? Or wishes you'd let them die?" He went down on one knee. "That's where I come in. After doctors like you cheat death, I give patients back their life."

The wind blew suddenly and he pulled up the collar of his leather jacket. "I help kids, Dad. The ones with facial trauma so acute that they have no prospects for a decent quality of life. Kids like Janie."

He smiled. "You know her. Cute little thing. Blond hair, blue eyes. Princess attitude. And her mom. Blond hair, brown eyes. Sexy, sassy and sweet in equal parts. Spine of steel and a heart of gold. A soft heart that's been stomped on one too many times, and that's sort of shut down her ability to trust. She's been abused by men who handed her hope, then snatched it away.

"You were there for her at a difficult time, Dad. Courtney appreciates it, by the way. But you're gone now and I'm going to—" Fill your shoes? Never in a million years, he thought. "I'm going to fix the damage to Janie's face. Then I'll go back to California. No excuse to stay after that."

The breeze stirred the tree branches above him and the rustling almost sounded like whispering. He heard the word *coward.* Or maybe he just felt like one.

He wasn't running away. He had a practice in California and people were counting on him. But who could he count on?

There was no little girl so happy to see him she raced into his arms to give him a hug, or chatter like a magpie about whatever was on her mind. No Courtney to tell about his day, make him laugh to take the edge off. Make love to. The familiar blackness opened up inside him. Except it wasn't familiar any more.

Since he'd come back to Walnut River, the empty feeling had disappeared. Janie and Courtney had moved into his heart and taken down the vacancy sign. But it would be up again soon when he went back to his glass-and-chrome life in Los Angeles. Compared to the warm, girly world he'd be leaving behind, it seemed cold and hollow and—not pink.

The breeze swirled through the trees and this time he swore there was a whisper. *Don't leave the woman you love.*

David wasn't sure if a soul had spoken or if the thought was simply there in his mind. He looked around, confirmed that he was still alone, kneeling by his father's grave. Maybe he should have been creeped out. Oddly enough, he wasn't.

"The thing is, Dad, I don't want to be another man who comes along and hurts Courtney. I care too much about her. Do no harm."

Don't leave the woman you love. He swore he heard the words again, and God, he was tempted. However the thought had come to him didn't make the reality of it any less true. Or any less complicated.

He'd fallen in love with Courtney.

The next morning before Janie's procedure, David went to see his brother. He knew Peter would be there early and it was the best time to talk, before patients demanded his attention.

He knocked, then entered the office where his big brother was doing paperwork. "Hi. Got a minute?"

Peter looked up and smiled with genuine pleasure. "Hey. Sure. Come in."

"Thanks." He took a chair in front of the desk.

"You're out and about early."

"I'm doing the reconstruction on Janie's face this morning."

Peter nodded. "How's Courtney holding up?"

"She's putting on a brave face for Janie, but she's scared."

"You look concerned. Is there reason to be?"

"Not about the surgery." David blew out a breath. "I care a lot about that little girl."

"And her mother?" Peter set his pen down and focused his full attention on the conversation.

"Yeah. Her mother, too."

"Is that going to affect your concentration in the O.R.?"

"You mean is my objectivity compromised?" David asked.

"Yeah. Something like that."

"I gave Janie my word that I'd make her look as good as new and I won't let her down. I'm very good at what I do. The truth is that I wouldn't trust her to anyone else."

"For you? Or for her mom?"

"For both of us."

"Wonders never cease," Peter said. "You're in love with Courtney Albright."

"What is this? Junior high?" They weren't kids any more, David thought. Dodging the truth was stupid. "Yeah. I am."

"When did this happen? How?"

"There's no procedure manual. No single moment when the clouds parted and the hand of God smacked me upside the head." He decided not to share his experience in the cemetery. Or his very real feeling that their father was somehow responsible for his epiphany. "It just happened."

"Congratulations. I couldn't be happier for you."

"Not so fast, bro. There's this small matter of the continental United States between us."

"A minor detail to be worked out."

"You think my work is minor?"

"Hardly. But people on the west coast aren't the only ones who can use your expertise." There was a gleam in his brother's eyes.

"Are you saying there'd be a place for me on staff here at Walnut River General?"

"That's exactly what I'm saying. Ella and I would both be giddy with joy if you came back."

"Giddy?" David's eyebrow rose as he fought the threatening grin. "I can see Ella giddy, maybe. But you?"

Peter shrugged. "Dad would be happy to know the prodigal son returned."

"I let him down, Peter. There's nothing I can do to change that. You'll never know how much I wish I could talk to him now—face to face—and make things okay between us. I wish I could hear him say he's proud of me."

Peter snapped his fingers. "That reminds me. I've got something for you."

"What?"

His brother reached into a drawer and pulled out a thick publication. "I was going through some of Dad's things and found this."

David reached across the desk and took the periodical—a medical journal. There was a sticky note marking a page. He opened the journal to the article he'd written about his positive results with scar-camouflage techniques and examples of successes in children from one of his trips to Nicaragua. The publication had come out in January, the month his dad had died. There was a note on the page in his father's handwriting.

He cleared his throat. "It says, 'Proud of David. Excellent work. Note to self—children make a liar out of you every time. Good excuse to call. About damn time.'"

After reading the words, David drew in a deep breath.

"What did he mean? About making a liar out of him?" Peter asked.

"I did something in college that I'm not very proud of." He met his brother's gaze. "No point in going into detail. But Dad found out. He said I was a disgrace to the Wilder name and wouldn't amount to anything."

"Ah."

"I never had the chance to tell him I was sorry, Peter."

"And he never got a chance to tell you he was wrong. Sounds like an even playing field to me." His brother glanced upward, then met his gaze again. "He knows, David. He's looking down on us right now and smiling and thinking his children are doing him proud. They're all together—"

David snapped his fingers. "You're not the only one who forgot something. I talked to Anna." Thoughts of Courtney had pushed everything else out of his mind.

"Our prodigal sister?"

"More than you know." David brushed his hand over his father's note. "She's working for Northeastern HealthCare, Peter."

"What?"

"The company trying to take over the hospital our father built. You remember."

"Of course I remember." Now he looked worried.

"What's wrong?" David asked.

"I just found out that the state attorney general's office is sending an investigator. There have been allegations and stories leaked to the press about the hospital. This investigator is supposed to dig through everything and separate fact, fiction and rumor."

"Is that a problem?"

"Any time a government agency does an inspection it's a problem. What makes it worse is that NHC wants this hospital. The question is how far they'll go to make the deal happen."

"You think they have someone on the inside here at the hospital?"

"Who knows?" Peter shrugged. "And I'm not sure that matters now. It's ugly and likely to get a lot worse. And it doesn't help that one of the Wilders works for them."

"Sorry to be the bearer of bad news." Especially when his brother had given him something so special. He closed the medical journal and felt a weight he hadn't been aware of lift from his heart.

"It's one of many reasons that I'm glad you'll be here to watch my back. I'll need all the help I can get to save the hospital."

"Count me in." David stood, magazine in hand. "Thanks for this. I have to get down to the O.R. I want Janie to know I'm there before they put her to sleep."

Peter nodded, then stood and held out his hand. "She's in excellent hands."

"Thanks." It meant a lot to have his brother's respect.

"Good luck."

"I thought you said she was in excellent hands."

"She is. And that's not what I meant. Good luck with Courtney."

From his mouth to God's ear. Maybe his dad could pull some strings up there because David needed all the help he could get. He had his doubts that Courtney would be willing to take one more chance on hope.

Especially when he was the man handing it to her.

Chapter Fifteen

In Walnut River General's second-floor lounge, reserved for family and friends of surgery patients, Courtney stared out the window, not really seeing much of anything. The room behind her was hospital-standard-issue—tweed chairs and a leather-padded bench along one wall. Magazines were scattered on tables and a TV was mounted in the corner, turned off at the moment. None of it took her mind off the fact that her baby was down the hall having an operation on her little face and the waiting was hell.

She remembered when David had told her the repair couldn't be done until the swelling subsided. She'd wondered how she was going to get through the wait because she so desperately wanted Janie well and back to normal, right then, right there. Somehow time *had* passed, relatively quickly and painlessly. If she admitted the truth to herself, the reason was David. He'd even made sure to be with them before Janie went to sleep. This was the day she'd been both anticipating and dreading and she trusted him absolutely with her child's welfare.

She'd been able to move forward and get through each day by leaning on him, looking forward to seeing him. Loving him.

In spite of her highly developed emotional defenses, the man had gone over, under, around and through them until she'd waved the white flag and fallen for him. Part of his reason for hanging around was to confront the demons she'd once accused him of having. She sincerely hoped that he'd found a measure of peace because he deserved it. Since their first meeting she'd wondered about the price of his generosity and knew now that it was going to cost her her heart and soul.

"Courtney, any news yet?"

She turned at the deep, familiar voice and saw Peter Wilder in the doorway. "Not yet. It's only been a little while. David said the procedure would take at least several hours."

"Janie's going to be fine." Peter walked over to her and put a comforting arm around her shoulders. So like his father. "My brother was a dweeb growing up, but he's matured since then and is a competent surgeon."

"Dweeb? Is that the official medical term?" she asked, looking up and smiling in spite of the situation.

He looked thoughtful. "Yes. But rest assured. There's every indication that he's left his dweeb days behind him."

It would never have occurred to her to call him a dweeb. Maybe hunk and hottie—even Janie knew that one. Sweetie. Steadfast. Compassionate. Caring. Complicated.

"So he probably wouldn't respond if I called him Dr. Dweeb?" she asked.

Peter's mouth curved upward in a smile. "Paging Dr. Dweeb. I like that."

He reminded her of David in a teasing mood and she could almost see the wheels turning.

"Don't you dare call him that," she warned. "And if you blame the nickname on me, I'll deny it."

"I could be bought off," he suggested, dark eyes twinkling. "Baked goods of any kind. Peanut butter cookies are especially effective in helping me keep mum."

"Because they stick to the roof of your mouth?" she suggested.

"Good one." He laughed.

"What?" Ella Wilder stood just inside the door.

"Did you know your brother is a sugar slut?" Courtney asked.

"His dirty little secret," Ella agreed. "He can be had for as little as a candy bar or scoop of ice cream. Absolutely shameful. And why are we going to give him a sugar rush?"

"Courtney doesn't want David to know she called him Dr. Dweeb."

"I did not!" she denied. "You're the one who said he wasn't so cool when he was a kid."

"That implies I think he's cool now," Peter commented thoughtfully. "I would never say such a thing."

"Merciful heavens, no," Ella said in mock seriousness. "The planet wouldn't be large enough to contain his ego."

Courtney smiled as the two of them good-naturedly bashed their brother, all in the pursuit of taking her mind off worrying about Janie. What a special family the Wilders were. When she missed their father, which was often, it brought her a measure of comfort to know that he'd raised his children to be considerate and caring human beings. That meant his kindness would live on.

"Any word on Janie?" Ella finally asked.

Courtney shook her head. "Not yet. But it hasn't been that long."

"You know," Ella said, "sometimes a procedure can take a little longer than estimated. We make educated guesses based on test results, but until we're there, we don't really know for sure what's going on."

"It doesn't mean there's anything wrong," Peter interjected. "Just that he has to see for himself what the situation is."

"That's what I just said." Ella glared, but there was a gleam in her eyes. "Just because I'm the youngest doesn't mean I'm incompetent."

"I never said you were, but if the stethoscope fits…" Peter looked at her and shrugged.

"I'll have you know—" She stopped, and wagged a finger. "I refuse to get sucked into an argument. Let me simply say that David's not the only one with ego issues. What is it with the Wilder men?"

"They're good and kind," Courtney said. "Caring enough to distract me. If you guys weren't here, I'd be a basket case."

Peter slid his hands into the pockets of his lab coat. "We aim to please. Patients aren't just the sum of their medical problem. They're flesh and blood and have families who worry. We look at healing through mind, body and spirit. Janie's going to need you most when she comes out of surgery. If your spirit is ailing, how can you take care of her?"

"How is she?" Elizabeth Albright walked in the room with her husband right behind her. "Is there any word on my granddaughter?"

"Not yet," Courtney said.

In her hands, the older woman carried a cardboard holder with a hot beverage cup and a bag. She held it out. "I brought you tea and a muffin."

"I couldn't eat anything—"

"You must keep up your strength," Elizabeth interrupted. "How can you take care of Janie if you're weak and undernourished?" She took Courtney's arm and steered her to a chair with a table beside it. "Come. Sit. Eat."

Morris Albright sat beside her. "She's not a puppy, Elizabeth."

"I know that. I'm just trying to help."

"I know." Courtney met her gaze. "Thank you."

"You're welcome." A small smile curved her mouth and softened the tension on her gently lined face. "We'd have been here sooner, but we stopped in the gift shop to order a balloon bouquet for Janie's room. While we were there, we took the liberty of making sure all was running smoothly in your absence. Everything seems under control."

"Karen assured me she'd take care of everything."

"That impossibly young girl we met?" Elizabeth asked.

"Yes. She works part-time. A college student." Courtney thought for a moment. "She's about the same age I was when I came to Walnut River."

Morris squeezed her hand. "We weren't there for you then, Courtney."

"I didn't mean— I was just commenting—"

"It's all right." He smiled. "We're here now. Better late than never."

"I appreciate it so much—" A multitude of emotions pressed on her chest and choked off her words.

She looked at them all. Peter. Ella. The Albrights. Tears gathered in her eyes.

Elizabeth pushed the muffin and tea out of the way and sat on the table since there was no chair available beside Courtney. She took Courtney's good hand between her own. "It's okay to cry, sweetheart. We're here to pick up the slack. You're not alone any more."

"The truth is I haven't really been alone since I came to Walnut River," she said, smiling through her tears. She glanced at Peter and Ella and thought again of James Wilder. "People who work here in the hospital are a tight-knit group and made me one of them right from the start." She looked at her in-laws, Janie's family. Her family, too. "And having you here means the world to me."

David was responsible for that. If he hadn't reached out, she'd have gone on assuming that they would reject her. She'd have deprived her child of the special relationship between granddaughter and grandparents.

Ella pulled a chair closer and sat in front of her. "Don't cry, Court. She's going to be the way she was before the accident."

"But will I?" The words slipped out before she could stop them. "And I don't mean that in a selfish way. But you can't go through a trauma like this and…meet the people you meet…and not be changed forever."

Peter walked closer, joining the little protective circle around her. "For what it's worth, David feels the same way."

"He's a nice man," she said, brushing more tears away when Elizabeth put an arm around her. "I'm grateful he put his west-coast life on hold to help Janie. He's probably anxious to get back."

"How do you feel about my brother, Courtney?" Peter slid his hands in his pockets.

Ella glared up at him. "That's an inappropriate question. I speak for the rest of the country when I say I'm glad you practice medicine and not diplomacy." She looked back at Courtney. "Don't answer that."

"She's right," Peter said. "It's none of my business. But I want you to think about something. When you see Janie's face after the surgery you're going to wonder if the reconstruction is a success, because it will look worse before it gets better."

"David warned me," Courtney said.

But she had a feeling Peter was talking about more than the surgery, trying to let her down easy and prepare her to be alone. She knew how to handle it because she'd been alone all her life. But it had been so much easier before she knew David.

He'd been there for her and she couldn't help being sad that he was going away. He was the kind of man who would take a lifetime to get to know, the kind of man who would never be boring. Part of her wanted to feel sorry for herself that he'd walked into her life and would walk out again taking her heart with him.

She would always remember him. He was one of the good guys and she was grateful to him for showing her they did exist.

When David walked into the lounge, everyone stood up as one. He looked tired, Courtney thought. And darn sexy in his blue scrubs.

"How's Janie?" she asked.

He stood in front of her and ran his fingers through his hair. "Still out from the anesthesia, but she'll be awake soon. The procedure went better than I could have hoped. We have to watch for infection. As with all invasive techniques, there will be a scar, but too small and inconspicuous to cause her any anxiety. Bottom line, I expect her to make a full recovery." Finally he grinned down at her.

After three beats of dead silence, everyone cheered, hugged and high-fived. Courtney buried her face in her hands and cried. Instantly she felt strong arms around her as she was folded against a wide chest that felt familiar and safe.

"Please don't cry, Courtney," David said.

"I cried when Peter and Ella came to sit with me. I blubbered when the Albrights showed up. I've cried so much there's a real danger of dehydration. Trust me, these are happy tears." Mostly. But some were because now he would be going home and she would miss him desperately. But there was no way she'd tell him that. "I feel like I've been crying for a month. Why stop now?"

"Because Janie needs you now."

So holding her wasn't personal; it was all about him being a doctor. She sniffled and lifted her head. Everyone else had quietly and tactfully left and now she was alone with David. His handsome image wavered through her tears.

"Just stop?" She struggled to put a teasing note in her voice. "Is that part of your bedside manner for dealing with a hysterical mother? If so, I have to tell you it needs work, doctor."

"I see no hysteria. And the scared, unhappy mother is you. Seeing you cry rips me up. I can't stand it."

"What?" Who knew shock, not dehydration, could dry up tears? When she tried to back up a step, he curved his fingers around her upper arms.

"I'm in love with you, Courtney."

She couldn't believe she'd heard right. Maybe all the crying had caused flooding that short-circuited her brain *and* her hearing. Surely he hadn't said he loved her. Maybe it was part of the Wilder family conspiracy to let her down easy. He could say it because he was leaving town and no follow-up would be required. He'd look like a hero, and there'd be no guilt to infect his conscience.

This time she pulled away. "That's just— You don't have to say that."

"Yeah, I do."

"And why's that?"

"Because you were right. My father would be deeply disappointed if I took away the wrong message from him loving a child." He blew out a long breath. "But it's not just about that. I've felt empty for a very long time. And now—"

"What?"

He shrugged. "I don't any more."

"Since when?" she asked.

"Since meeting you. And Janie." He glanced toward the window for a moment, then looked back. "I didn't hang around because I needed a vacation from work. It's because I was emotionally spent. I had nothing, no one to fill up the void. You and Janie got to me in a way no one ever has."

She stared at him. "It was the bump on my head, wasn't it? You're a sucker for a woman with a broken wrist and a concussion."

"Joke if you want—"

"I don't need your permission. Humor has gotten me around every lousy pothole on this road we call life. I'm not about to stop now."

"Good. I think it's that sassy, in-your-face attitude that first made me fall in love with you."

"Not the contusion?" she asked in a small voice.

"No." His mouth curved up, then he got serious. Cupping her face in his hands, he kissed her softly. "It was the combination of sarcasm and the unconditional and bottomless love for your child that I fell for."

"I'm not sure I know how to respond to that."

He brushed his thumb across her mouth, then dropped his hands. "You could start by saying you love me, too."

"How do you know I do?"

"I know."

"Dr. Hottie strikes again?"

"Courtney—"

She sighed. "I'm not sure what good it will do for me to say it."

"Why?"

"Okay, if I have to give you a geography lesson, I will. I live here in Walnut River. East coast. And you live—" With her finger, she made an arc in the air to the left, indicating the entire continental United States. "All the way on the other side of the country. West coast."

"So?"

"Okay. Now we'll have a lesson in relationships doomed

to failure. You have an enormously profitable medical practice in California that you've been neglecting."

"I love you. That's more important than an address."

She ignored that although her heart started pounding. The man had gifted hands and a silver tongue. And she wasn't sure why she was resisting, except that self-preservation instincts were a hard habit to break.

"When you go back, you'll have every intention of making it work with me. We'll promise to take long weekends, get together every chance we get. But you'll get involved with your patients. I'm busy with work, getting my degree and raising Janie. She's got school, which narrows our window of opportunity to be around her holidays. Eventually we'll move on." She shrugged. "I think it would be easier if I just move on now."

"Easier for who?" His eyes narrowed. "I know you've taken some hits in life, but it never crossed my mind that the gutsy woman I met in the E.R. was a coward."

"I'm not." But the accusation hit a nerve.

"Then why are you giving up without a fight?"

"Because the only way we'll work is if I give up my life." The tears threatened again. "Only an idiot would expect you to sacrifice a lucrative medical practice and I can't give up what I've built here."

"I love you. I want you to be happy. I—"

She put her fingers to his lips to silence him. "You have to understand, David. I raised myself. I didn't grow up with anything resembling a family. When I came to Walnut River, I was pregnant and scared. Janie was born in this hospital. It's the heart and soul of this town thanks to your father. He gave me a job and I was determined not to let him down. So I worked hard. The silver lining was that I made friends. Put down roots. This is more than a town to me. It's the first and only family I've ever had. It's part of my heart."

"I understand."

"Do you?"

"Yeah. It's part of my heart, too, and the reason I came back." He searched her eyes. "But I'd still like an answer. If we'd met in the elevator of our mutual condo complex in Los Angeles, would you be afraid to tell me how you feel?"

"Yes." She shook her head. "No. It's just so hard to be this close to everything you've ever wanted, you know? What if I reach out and it all falls apart? If the worst-case scenario happens—"

Then she remembered what Peter had said about things getting worse before they got better. When David went back to his life would she hurt any less if she never told him how she felt?

With her knuckle, she brushed away a single tear that slid down her cheek. Then she looked into his blue eyes and her mouth trembled. "I love you. Are you happy now?"

"I will be if you'll agree to marry me."

"But—"

This time he put his fingers to her lips. "The thing is, it's fortunate that you're happy living in Walnut River because I'm going to be living here too. I accepted a position on staff at the hospital and plan to move my practice here. I've missed the town and my family."

"Let me get this straight. You're giving up your life for me?"

"I'm not giving up anything," he countered. "And I'm getting everything. For the record, my reasons are completely selfish because living without you and Janie isn't living at all. I love you, Court. I love your strength and stubbornness, although not at the moment because I'm not fond of suspense when everything I've ever wanted hangs in the balance. Just say you'll marry me."

In the end it was easy. A no-brainer.

"Okay." Her heart was so full, she'd never imagined it was possible to be this happy. "I would love to marry you."

He kissed her then snuggled her against him. "We'll have to go tell Janie." There was a hint of nervousness in his voice, an indication of how deeply he cared for her little girl.

"You know she wants you to be her dad, Dr. David." Courtney managed to skip words past the lump of emotion in her throat.

"I'd like nothing better."

"Life is funny," she whispered, blinking back tears. "When your sister paged you to come and examine my daughter, I knew I'd be getting a famous physician, but I had no idea that doctor would turn out to be a daddy, too."

And the man who would make all her dreams come true.

* * * * *

Look for the next chapter in the new
Special Edition continuity
THE WILDER FAMILY

When a one-night stand leads to a surprise pregnancy,
E.R. nurse Simone Garner tries to navigate a relationship
with the eager daddy-in-waiting. But as pressure mounts
from the impending takeover, can she handle a
fairy-tale romance—with a younger man?

Don't miss
ONCE UPON A PREGNANCY
By Judy Duarte
On sale April 2008,
wherever Silhouette Books are sold.

Enjoy a sneak preview of
MATCHMAKING WITH A MISSION
by B.J. Daniels,
part of the WHITEHORSE, MONTANA *miniseries.*
Available from Harlequin Intrigue
in April 2008.

Nate Dempsey has returned to Whitehorse to uncover the truth about his past...

Nate sensed someone watching the house and looked out in surprise to see a woman astride a paint horse just on the other side of the fence. He quickly stepped back from the filthy second-floor window, although he doubted she could have seen him. Only a little of the June sun pierced the dirty glass to glow on the dust-coated floor at his feet as he waited a few heartbeats before he looked out again.

The place was so isolated he hadn't expected to see another soul. Like the front yard, the dirt road was waist-high with weeds. When he'd broken the lock on the back door, he'd had to kick aside a pile of rotten leaves that had blown in from last fall.

As he sneaked a look, he saw that she was still there,

staring at the house in a way that unnerved him. He shielded his eyes from the glare of the sun off the dirty window and studied her, taking in her head of long blond hair that feathered out in the breeze from under her Western straw hat.

She wore a tan canvas jacket, jeans and boots. But it was the way she sat astride the brown-and-white horse that nudged the memory.

He felt a chill as he realized he'd seen her before. In that very spot. She'd been just a kid then. A kid on a pretty paint horse. Not this one—the markings were different. Anyway, it couldn't have been the same horse, considering the last time he had seen her was more than twenty years ago. That horse would be dead by now.

His mind argued it probably wasn't even the same girl. But he knew better. It was the way she sat the horse, so at home in a saddle and secure in her world on the other side of that fence.

To the boy he'd been, she and her horse had represented freedom, a freedom he'd known he would never have—even after he escaped this house.

Nate saw her shift in the saddle, and for a moment he feared she planned to dismount and come toward the house. With Ellis Harper in his grave, there would be little to keep her away.

To his relief, she reined her horse around and rode back the way she'd come.

As he watched her ride away, he thought about the way she'd stared at the house—today and years ago. While the smartest thing she could do was to stay clear of this house, he had a feeling she'd be back.

Finding out her name should prove easy, since he figured she must live close by. As for her interest in Harper House… He would just have to make sure it didn't become a problem.

* * * * *

Be sure to look for
MATCHMAKING WITH A MISSION
and other suspenseful Harlequin Intrigue stories,
available in April
wherever books are sold.

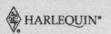

REQUEST YOUR FREE BOOKS!

2 FREE NOVELS PLUS 2 FREE GIFTS!

SPECIAL EDITION®

Life, Love and Family!

YES! Please send me 2 FREE Silhouette Speãal Edition® novels and my 2 FREE gifts (gifts are worth about $10). After receiving them, if I don't wish to receive any more books, I can return the shipping statement marked "cancel." If I don't cancel, I will receive 6 brand-new novels every month and be billed just $4.24 per book in the U.S. or $4.99 per book in Canada, plus 25¢ shipping and handling per book and applicable taxes, if any*. That's a savings of at least 15% off the cover price! I understand that accepting the 2 free books and gifts places me under no obligation to buy anything. I can always return a shipment and cancel at any time. Even if I never buy another book from Silhouette, the two free books and gifts are mine to keep forever.

235 SDN EEYU 335 SDN EEY6

Name _____ (PLEASE PRINT)

Address _____ Apt. #

City _____ State/Prov. _____ Zip/Postal Code

Signature (if under 18, a parent or guardian must sign)

Mail to the **Silhouette Reader Service:**
IN U.S.A.: P.O. Box 1867, Buffalo, NY 14240-1867
IN CANADA: P.O. Box 609, Fort Erie, Ontario L2A 5X3

Not valid to current subscribers of Silhouette Speãal Edition books.

Want to try two free books from another line?
Call 1-800-873-8635 or visit www.morefreebooks.com.

* Terms and prices subject to change without notice. N.Y. residents add applicable sales tax. Canadian residents will be charged applicable provinãal taxes and GST. This offer is limited to one order per household. All orders subject to approval. Credit or debit balances in a customer's account(s) may be offset by any other outstanding balance owed by or to the customer. Please allow 4 to 6 weeks for delivery. Offer available while quantities last.

Your Privacy: Silhouette is committed to protecting your privacy. Our Privacy Policy is available online at www.eHarlequin.com or upon request from the Reader Service. From time to time we make our lists of customers available to reputable third parties who may have a product or service of interest to you. If you would prefer we not share your name and address, please check here. ☐

SSE08

SAVE $1.00

New York Times BESTSELLING AUTHOR

SHERRYL WOODS

Family crises, old flames and returning home… Hannah Matthews and Luke Stevens discover that sometimes the unexpected is just what it takes to start over…and to heal the heart.

∞ *Seaview Inn* ∞

"Flesh-and-blood characters, terrific dialogue and substantial stakes…"
—*Publishers Weekly* on *A Slice of Heaven*

SHERRYL WOODS

On sale March 2008!

SAVE $1.00

on the purchase price of SEAVIEW INN by Sherryl Woods.

Offer valid from March 1, 2008, to May 31, 2008.
Redeemable at participating retail outlets. Limit one coupon per purchase.

52608272

5 65373 00076 2   (8100) 0 11475

® and TM are trademarks owned and used by the trademark owner and/or its licensee.
© 2008 Harlequin Enterprises Limited

MSW2529CPN

nocturne™

The Bloodrunners
trilogy continues with book #2.

The hunt meant more to Jeremy Burns than dominance—
it meant facing the woman he left behind. Once
Jillian Murphy had belonged to Jeremy, but now she was
the Spirit Walker to the Silvercrest wolves. It would take
more than the rights of nature for Jeremy to renew his
claim on her—and she would not go easily once he had.

LAST WOLF
HUNTING

by RHYANNON BYRD

Available in April wherever books are sold.

Be sure to watch out for the last book,
Last Wolf Watching, **available in May.**

SN61785